LEGE

The Witch's Cookbook

Raeka + Torrin,
Remember, sometimes
monsters are real!
Hope you enjoy.
Taylor Pensoneau

TAYLOR PENSONEAU

Legend Hollow:
The Witch's Cookbook

Illustration By
Elise Pensoneau

Cover Design
Lily Uivel

Cover Inspiration
Lana Pensoneau

**Hallow House
Press**

HALLOW HOUSE PRESS

Santa Rosa Beach, FL

Copyright © 2023 by Taylor Pensoneau

Summary: When the magical Witch's Cookbook goes missing from the Rip Van Winkel Bakery, Elise, Coop and her brother Stephen must recover it from dark forces to save the bakery, their town and even possibly themselves.

[1. Fantasy Magical Realism-Fiction. 2. Children's and teen spooky/horror-Fiction. 3. Coming of Age-Fiction.]

ISBN: 9798857608661

For Mom and Dad, who passed on the creativity and drive to make writing possible

CONTENTS

PROLOGUE

From the journal of Edmund Vander Poel, High Doctor, October
Society of New York City

October 28, 1806, Upstate New York, Hudson Valley

*R*eports have come to me of increased activity of the fiendish
type on the outskirts of Gould Hollow (commonly referred to
as Legend Hollow due to the many mysterious goings-on) during
recent witching hours. Said increases have coincided with the
beginning of the full moon phase. I have myself witnessed ghosts
and banshees shrieking in the trees and suspected November Men
stalking the shadows. The October Society has formed circles of
fellowship deep in the hollows, attended by high doctors, Indian
wizards, and certain allied witches' covens gathering to protect
the citizens from these unnatural forces.

*The inhabitants of so-called Legend Hollow have suffered
an awful fright from these sights and have chosen to close their*

shutters at nightfall and shelter at their hearths till morning. The spooks' midnight jamborees have garnered the attention of others in the valley and beyond. One such person is Washington Irving, who my associates tell me traveled from New York City with two prizes in mind.

Firstly, Washington Irving is a man seeking to craft tales of what goes on in the night. He is accumulating knowledge, chronicling lore, and listening to tales of bewitchings from the local Dutch settlers, freedmen, and Indians who make their home in the shadows of the Catskill Mountains. Yes, nearby Sleepy Hollow, Sunnyside, and other villages of the Hudson Valley can offer fodder aplenty for a man seeking material to put upon the page, but Mr. Irving had a second reason for his journey to Legend Hollow—some would argue a greater reason.

Whispers carried through the trees from the Valley all the way to New York City, say that the more compelling reason Mr. Irving traveled this direction was the fair Lana Holland, a denizen of Legend Hollow, and unbeknownst to Mr. Irving, a member of the Ember Coven and a witch of some renown. By all accounts the young writer has fallen for her in the hardest way be it a hex, a charm or simple nature one cannot say.

CHAPTER ONE

The Rip Van Winkle Bakery

From the journal of Niles Folsom, High Doctor, October Society of
New York City
Monday, October 26, 1986, Legend Hollow, New York

*L*egend Hollow finds itself in high spirits as All Hallows Eve
approaches. Images of witches, pumpkins, and goblins adorn
houses, and from the town's trees and lampposts hang legions
of monsters and spooks. Good feelings aside, it has been two
months since Marjorie Hopper of the Ember Coven disclosed the
unexplained disappearance of Washington Irving's Cookbook,
raising the collective concern of the Society.

The missing tome is significant as it contains more than two
hundred years of Mr. Irving's and his successors' documentation
of legends, spells, and recipes (yes, magical recipes, thanks to the

lovely Miss Holland) of the Hudson Valley. As one could imagine, this knowledge would be most dangerous in the wrong hands. Right on cue, there has been an increase of reported bewitchings, bumps in the night, and terrible frights not seen or heard of in over 150 years.

A bell rang out at Hay-Edwards School, signaling the end of the day. For a brief moment, the main doors of the old building remained closed, the schoolyard peaceful. That peace lasted a full twenty seconds until hundreds of students, kindergarten through eighth grade, burst outside from every exit.

Elise Wood hurried down the front steps of the main building. A gust of wind blew her ponytail to the side as her breath puffed white in the chill air. Five days until Halloween, and the seasons were making a serious change. It was about time that the weather got in on the act, she thought.

For several weeks already, the town had fully embraced autumn and all things spooky as the big day approached. Yellow and red leaves covered the school yard, and images of pumpkin-headed scarecrows, headless horsemen, and wicked witches hung from the wrought iron fence in front of the school.

Elise shuffled through the gathered leaves, enjoying their bright colors and the crackling sounds they made beneath her feet. At the school grounds' edge, she waited for her brother, Stephen, hoping Coop would be with him. Coop—short for Charles Fenimore Cooper—was in Elise's eighth-grade class and her best friend since kindergarten.

She spotted Coop first and fell in next to him as he ambled by, his nose buried in an open book. Only his jet-black hair appeared above the cover. Today's distraction was a Dungeons & Dragons Monster Manual.

"Hey, Coop," she said.

He gave her a quick nod and continued reading. Coop was Seneca Tribe, Haudenosaunee (Iroquois), one of the original Six Nations.

Amazing he never walks into a tree reading like that, Elise thought as she stepped over a crack.

"Watch out." She warned.

"My Indian senses guide me." He said as he navigated around the crack without looking up from his reading.

Nonsense, as usual, Elise thought.

"Elise, wait up!" Stephen came panting up behind to join them for the twelve-block walk home. His violin case bumped along the ground at the end of one of his long arms.

"Don't drag your violin," Elise scolded.

"I'm not," Stephen said, hoisting the instrument onto his shoulder.

Their path took them down Washington Street, the main thoroughfare of the town. Many storefronts along the way stood empty or abandoned, but Elise didn't focus on them. It was October, it was Halloween. Before her father had disappeared, it had been his favorite season, and she had shared that passion with him.

Other stores were decorated in the full spirit of the season. They passed Ichabod's Home and Auto Insurance, which had a giant stuffed headless horseman on the lawn. A sign on the horse read don't lose your head—renew your insurance policy now.

A block later came the Washington Supermarket. Bins with piles of pumpkins placed near the sidewalk teetered perilously high, threatening to catch the unaware in an orange avalanche. Elise couldn't resist running a hand over one pumpkin as they passed, inhaling the earthy smell of so many together in one place.

George First, another member of the Six Nations, swept the area around the front door. He had long, braided hair salted with grey running down the back of his shirt.

George shook his head at Elise's flirtation with danger but said nothing. He never spoke, as far as she knew. He wasn't a member of Coop's Seneca tribe and had a reputation for being strange. Coop always steered clear of him, saying that George First fashioned himself as a holy man or wizard or something.

He went back to his sweeping but kept an eye on the kids. He always seemed to be watching. Elise's father had known George and said he was alright, but he made Elise uneasy.

Next, they passed the police station. The front lawn swayed with flying witches handcuffed to tree branches. Finally, they reached the Irving movie theater.

"Oh, man, look at that! They're doing a scary movie marathon this weekend," Stephen said as he pointed at the theaters marquee.

Two blocks from home, Elise stopped in front of a two-story building. A sign read the rip van winkle bakery in small, scrolled letters. Hand-painted words decorated the large window, reading bewitchingly baked goods and enchanted confections served for over thirty years.

The building's roofline sagged with neglect. Elise often thought it was like an old man letting out a long sigh in the final years of his life.

"See you at school tomorrow," Coop said, without looking

up.

"Don't forget our ideas for the science fair are due," Elise said.

"Uh huh," Coop replied, continuing on his way.

Stephen waved to her and trotted after Coop, his violin case scraping the ground once more.

Elise pushed open the bakery's faded yellow door. The smell of warm bread and sugar washed over her, along with the herbal scents of thyme, lavender, and something wonderful she could not quite place. She grabbed an apron from a hook and walked past empty booths and tables to the main bakery case. This was always a highlight of her job. What creations had Ms. Hopper come up with today? Drum roll, she thought, as she scanned the case.

The usual cream puffs and pastries clustered on the bottom rows while the daily features adorned the top shelf. Today there were several standouts with handwritten labels. Great pumpkin turnovers with brandy cream sauce one label read. Mint witch cake pops read another at the front of a tray of treats shaped like witch's broomsticks. Old country bavarian strawberry creme strudel yet another label read. It sat in front of a row of tiny cakes topped with gnome hats made of colorful icing. Finally, squeezed in at the end of the case was something called Goblin Market bread crisps with peaches and thyme seasoning.

Mmm. Ms. Hopper's best effort this week. The quality of the pastries had been inconsistent and slipping over the last several months. It was refreshing to see such a creative explosion, and Elise's mouth began to water.

Ms. Hopper burst through a swinging door behind the counter, carrying a tray piled high with more Goblin Market bread crisps. A long, flowing purple dress swished around her tall, slender frame, and her grey hair was piled up like a tower on top of her head. Elise was always reminded of the leaning Tower of Pisa when she saw Ms. Hopper's hair teetering to and fro as she floated around the bakery seemingly effortlessly despite being in her eighties.

Lilah, her pet corgi, trotted closely behind, always underfoot. The dog was all ears and head with legs no more than a few inches long. She trotted past Elise with a woof of acknowledgment on her way to her bed in the corner.

"Well, good afternoon, Elise."

"Hi, Ms. Hopper. How was the morning business?"

"Zip-a-dee, dip-a-dee, we had a good morning! We sold dozens of the crisps." A smile spread across her face but then vanished. "Luckily, I can still remember the Goblin Market crisp recipe even if the others are beginning to fade from the old noggin." She tapped a long, slender finger to her forehead. "I just wish I could remember where I placed Mr. Irving and Aunt Lana's Cookbook. Oh, snookidee dookitee."

Elise had grown accustomed to Ms. Hopper's quirks and barely even noticed the rhyming words anymore. They were just gibberish anyway. But she did roll her eyes at the mention of the Cookbook.

Elise's father, a professor of literature at the local college, had been an expert on Washington Irving and his works such as "The Legend of Sleepy Hollow" and "Rip Van Winkle," and he had never mentioned that Washington Irving had written a cookbook. Nor could he even prove, despite his best efforts, that Washington Irving had ever actually visited Legend Hollow.

But Elise's curiosity had been raised the first time she

had seen Ms. Hopper flipping through what she called the Cookbook. It had an aged brown leather cover with a large cake and, oddly, a black cauldron drawn on the front. When Elise had asked if she could look through it, Ms. Hopper's face had broken into a gentle smile.

"These aren't just recipes, these are bewitchments, enchantments, and spells, if you will, gathered over hundreds of years from the folk inhabiting these lands. Only a witch or high doctor can read these writings. Plus, pippity dippity, some of these spells and writings can be truly dangerous in the wrong hands."

Ms. Hopper then went back to reading from the ancient book. It was not until much later that it occurred to Elise that Ms. Hopper was reading the words and letters just fine.

The librarian at Elise's school had laughed when she asked if they had a copy of Washington Irving's Cookbook or knew anything about it. Embarrassed, she had given up inquiring further and chalked it up to just another quirk of Ms. Hopper, a woman given to fantasy if not outright odd behavior once in a while.

Lana Holland, Ms. Hopper's great-great-great-aunt, had been a real person. That much Elise knew from her dad. Miss Holland's family had been among the earliest settlers of Legend Hollow. Maybe she had written the Cookbook, but Elise suspected that the Washington Irving stuff was nonsense.

She felt a twinge of guilt at that thought. After all, her father had been devoted to Washington Irving's works and had been convinced, as had Ms. Hopper, that Washington Irving had spent significant time in Legend Hollow despite the often-expressed views of those living outside the city limits of Legend Hollow that he had never actually visited the small town.

"Why don't you restock the top shelf, grab a pastry, and then get your homework started?" Ms. Hopper suggested.

"Sure, Ms. Hopper." There were no customers in the shop at the moment, and if recent history was any indicator, there wouldn't be many more as the afternoon wore on.

After restocking, Elise cracked open her science book but had a hard time concentrating. The empty tables and lack of business weighed on her mind. What would happen to the shop—and Ms. Hopper—if business didn't pick up?

In the past, the bakery had been wildly successful despite itself. The Hoppers had done no advertising, and the tiny basement shop huddled in a nook, nearly hidden from the main street was difficult to find, but it simply hadn't mattered. The enchanted puffs and airy pastries whipped customers into a frenzy. Soon after its opening, news of the shop had spread like wildfire throughout the town.

Seven days a week, people had shown up as early as 5:30 a.m. to try the new concoctions. Each morning offered new wonders such as Bewitched Cheesecakes, Troll's Toe Figs, and Apricot Kuchens imbued with elven rosemary-pine spirit. Lines had snaked around the block and been so long that while people waited, friendships had been struck up, dates made, and future husbands and wives first introduced.

Elise's dad had read aloud newspaper reviews showering praise upon the bakery. They often tried to get to the root of what made the place great but never could put their finger on it. Did the secret lie in the vast collection of ingredients partially visible in the back room? Customers could see dozens of jars with labels like enchanted rose petals, backwoods basil, moonlight lavender, tricky thyme, rosemary of the hollow, and yet others whose names they could not quite make out from their vantage point.

Eventually, Elise and her dad gave up trying to figure it out and simply got in line like everyone else. Her dad brought her most every weekend like clockwork and even some weekdays. Those were the moments she missed the most after his disappearance.

She tried to shake off the memory and get to her homework, but it wasn't going to happen. Instead, she watched Ms. Hopper entertain a lone customer. She was an older woman, a regular, who surveyed the display cases.

"How are we today, Ms. Thorstad? Are we hunky dory?" Ms. Hopper slid some Enchanted Sleep Peach Dumplings in her direction.

"Oh, decent enough. I noticed the woods felt a bit out of balance today, but hopefully it will even itself out soon enough," Ms. Thorstad responded.

Elise rolled her eyes again. She found Ms. Thorstad nearly as strange as Ms. Hopper. She liked to wear similar long, flowing dresses and never flinched at Ms. Hopper's strange comments, often matching them with her own oddities.

"I noticed you were a little stressed recently, so I had my assistants make some dumplings. Give you a little bumpity mumpity." Ms. Hopper winked. "I added brandy and pixie cream sauce for you. Mr. Irving's Cookbook used to say that the dumplings were good for relaxation. Who am I to argue?"

"Yes, yes." Ms. Thorstad nodded. "You're probably right. I'll take two orders. Just wrap them up for me. I'll eat them at home with a little extra brandy sauce, if you know what I mean."

Ms. Hopper winked again and packed the dumplings in a tiny white cardboard box. She tied it up with a bow and stood back to admire her work before handing the box to Ms. Thorstad.

When interacting with her customers, Ms. Hopper came alive, but otherwise she seemed to be getting very forgetful and absent-minded. Her decline started when she turned eighty and had only gotten worse since her husband Lynn passed away the year before. Losing her Cookbook had only made matters worse. Without it, she had forgotten portions of her recipes or entire recipes altogether.

After Lynn's death, she spent weeks looking for the lost Cookbook. She wondered aloud if Lynn had taken it with him to the grave. She had often said that it would be just like him to misplace it by accident.

As Elise had watched the bakery slide downhill, the stories Ms. Hopper told about Aunt Holland, kobolds, goblins, spirits, and witches lost their charm and began to irritate her. Ms. Hopper was still able to conjure baked magic on some days, and Elise had more patience with it all then, but on the days Ms. Hopper struggled with the recipes, Elise's patience wore thin. Stretching strings across doorways to keep out trolls, singing to keep her assistants, the kobolds, in a good mood, and other eccentric behavior began to wear down Elise as the shop's customers slipped away.

She was glad to be distracted by the whiskered face of Jonathan Hernandez peering in through the front door. Mr. Hernandez served as the landlord, maintenance man, and Johnny-on-the-spot for the two-story building housing the bakery. Although he didn't own the space where the bakery and Ms. Hopper resided, he owned the rest of the building and didn't seem to mind helping out when he could.

A large key ring hanging from his tool belt jangled as Mr. Hernandez entered the shop. Ms. Hopper declared that it was his way of announcing his presence to any lurking evil spirits when he entered a room. It was his signature whether he liked it or not, Elise thought.

"Any more of that Goblin Market Crisp left? I think I need a second helping," Mr. Hernandez said.

"Of course." Ms. Hopper smiled. She quickly wrapped another box with the same flourish and pushed it across the counter. "No charge. I will be closing in a couple of hours anyway."

"Oh no, Ms. Hopper, that's not necessary." Mr. Hernandez looked around the empty room and nodded a hello to Elise. "I'm more than happy to pay."

"No," Ms. Hopper said. "Remember, you fixed the clogged drains for free last week, so it's freezy deezy."

"Oh, that was nothing. Just a matter of removing the wooden doll shoes and clothing that were clogging it up." He muttered, shooting a glance over towards Elise.

"Oh, the kobolds are such messy folk." She shook her head.

"The Kobolds, huh?"

"Yes, you know my assistants." Ms. Hopper said in a matter of fact fashion.

"Uh huh." Mr. Hernandez said as he clanged over to the counter for his box. "Well, you let me know the next time you need something done around here, and I'll get it taken care of in a jiffy."

"Well, actually there is something you can do for me," Ms. Hopper said.

"Sure, Ms. Hopper."

"I just whipped up a sample of our headliner for tomorrow, and I need your opinion." She grabbed a tray from behind the counter and extended it in Mr. Hernandez's direction.

"You too, Elise—come over and try one. I call them the Wizard's Cauldron. They're a crème Brulé topped with a mini wizard's hat dipped in fairy dust sugar."

Mr. Hernandez grabbed a sample and eagerly popped it into his mouth. Elise was about to do the same when she saw Mr. Hernandez's face screw up painfully. Elise discreetly put her treat back on the tray as he spat out the dessert into his hand.

"Ms. Hopper. This dessert is not right!" He dragged a forearm across his thick mustache and mouth.

Ms. Hopper raised her eyebrows and set the tray down. She picked up one of her Wizard's Cauldrons and gave it a sniff.

"Hmph—smells like I used salt instead of sugar for the fairy dust. It's so difficult to get it right without my book." She took a tentative bite. "Oh, hogelly mogelly, and that hat isn't made of chocolate, that's for sure."

"It isn't?" A hint of concern replaced the look of pain on Mr. Hernandez's face. "Well, what is it then?" He glanced down at his hand.

Ms. Hopper sniffed again. "Oh." She let out a small laugh.

"Well, what is it?"

"Apparently I made the mini hats with the chopped liver I had planned to use for Lilah's doggy treats."

Elise edged farther away from the tray. Chopped liver? How had Ms. Hopper gotten the recipe so wrong? Meanwhile, at the mention of her name, Lilah had trotted over, ears perked up. She sniffed the air and searched the room for the source of the chopped liver smell. Ms. Hopper tossed the tiny wizard hat to the corgi, who swallowed it in one gulp.

"Buck up, you'll be fine," Ms. Hopper said at the look of concern still adorning Mr. Hernandez's face. "It's simply an early Halloween trick instead of a treat." She shook her head and took the tray back to the kitchen.

Mr. Hernandez shot Elise a look of concern this time, which she returned. At this pace the shop wouldn't even make it to Halloween.

TAYLOR PENSONEAU

CHAPTER TWO

Dr. Grout

It was an hour before closing time, and Elise was finishing the final sweeping for the day. Mr. Hernandez had returned to the shop for his evening coffee and sat scratching Lilah's ears. The corgi rolled onto her back and made her belly available.

Ms. Hopper took several of the unsold pastries and put them into a brown bag with the name George written on it. It was for George First, who usually picked them up in the morning for breakfast on his way to work at the Washington Market. Elise liked that Ms. Hopper still did these kinds of things despite the bakery's problems, but she was still worried.

From time to time, Elise looked up from her sweeping and glanced over at Mr. Hernandez, who shot back concerned looks from under his bushy eyebrows. He was worried too.

"Oh, for gosh mcgosh sake, will the two of you cut it out,"

LEGEND HOLLOW: THE WITCH'S COOKBOOK 21

Ms. Hopper scolded.

"But—" Mr. Hernandez began.

"I'm fine! It was just a simple mistake with the ingredients."

"I get that, but—" Before Mr. Hernandez could continue, the doorbell tinkled and the door swung open.

A heavy man in a three-piece suit waddled inside. The clothing, all three pieces of it, could barely contain his round shape.

"Hello, Ms. Hopper," the man said.

"How can we help you, Dr. Grout?" Ms. Hopper threw her cleaning rag down on the counter. Her flair had evaporated.

He walked across the room with short, purposeful strides, then stopped to lean on the back of a chair. It creaked under the strain as if it would collapse at any moment. Elise feared that Dr. Grout's great stomach would pull him over onto his face.

As far as she knew, Dr. Grout was not a medical doctor but something Ms. Hopper called a developer and an investor. Ms. Hopper had told Elise that he'd long had his eye on the building and the entire block it sat upon. He envisioned a complex of storage units going up in the area.

Mr. Hernandez's building and Ms. Hopper's bakery within it were the final holdouts. Only the two of them had refused to sell, and Dr. Grout came by often to pressure them. Elise felt sick when she thought of Ms. Hopper and the bakery going away.

"Fear not, I do not come to talk business but only for desserts," Dr. Grout said, seemingly sensing Elise's thoughts. He hoisted himself up off of the chair and moved to the display case. "Hmm, I was a little disappointed by the Caramel Spider Scones the other day, but maybe the crêpes will make up for it."

"How many would you like?" Ms. Hopper asked while examining her fingernails.

"Oh, two should be sufficient."

Ms. Hopper handed him his box, thanked him, and said nothing more.

"Thank you, Ms. Hopper," Dr. Grout said with an exaggerated wave. He began waddling for the door but paused, looking back over his shoulder.

"I do hope these are better than the ones I tried last week. Word on the street is that you are slipping." He smiled, showing all of his teeth. "You can't afford to lose any more customers, I would think." He looked about the nearly empty shop. "A couple more weeks like this, and I imagine you would have to shut down, perhaps even sell."

"We're not closing anything, Dr. Grout!" Elise said, her temper rising. She knew she shouldn't speak to an adult in that tone, but she'd had enough of him harassing Ms. Hopper and Mr. Hernandez.

"Hmm, is that so?"

Elise squirmed as Dr. Grout turned his smile on her. He seemed momentarily lost in thought while still holding the door open. If only he would leave!

"You know what? I forget to get something for my friend James. How rude of me." Dr. Grout turned to look out the door. "James, come in and see what there is to eat," he called.

The doorway darkened as a large man filled the opening. His eyes were narrow above a long, bent nose. His shaggy black hair seemed to stand up in every direction, and more unruly hair protruded from his ears. He wore an ill-fitting yellow T-shirt along with what appeared to be snow pants.

James scanned the room for a moment before setting his gaze on Lilah and taking a step in her direction. Elise shrank back behind her broom as he approached, his strides clumsy and uneven. His upper body barely moved at all while his long arms hung almost motionless at his sides. A strong odor wafted from him, and Elise scrunched her nose. It reminded her of the greasy teenage boys who hung out in the back room of Aladdin's Castle arcade.

Lilah jumped from her bed and began to bark loudly at the lumbering man. She bared her teeth and raised the hair on her back.

"You get away from that dog!" Ms. Hopper shouted, grabbing another nearby broom.

Elise jumped at the ferocity of Ms. Hopper's reaction. Her voice was high and shaky. Was she . . . afraid? An involuntary quiver went through Elise as the large man's attention turned to Ms. Hopper.

He only looked at her briefly before turning his long, twisted nose up toward the ceiling. He began sniffing the air while Lilah barked at his feet. He ignored the barking and continued to sniff, his nostrils twitching with each deep breath. Eventually, the sniffing led him toward the bakery counter.

He quickened his pace to a jog, his snow pants swishing. Just as quickly as he had begun to run, he came to an abrupt stop at the display case, tilting his shaggy head side to side, pointing his nose toward the room behind the kitchen.

"Eat!" he yelled in a booming voice that made Elise jump again. He was winding his large body back into motion when a whirl of grey hair, a long purple dress, and a sturdy broom stopped him. Ms. Hopper stood before him, heaving with the effort.

"Be off!" she shouted. "You are not welcome here. Your invitation is revoked!"

Mr. Hernandez leaped from his booth and ran to Ms. Hopper's side, his key ring jangling away like an alarm bell. James paid no attention to Mr. Hernandez as he loomed over Ms. Hopper's thin frame. Elise stood frozen. Why hadn't she just kept her mouth shut earlier and not said anything?

"James." Dr. Grout said evenly, the smile still on his face. "It appears you are not welcome here. Let's be off. We can visit again another time."

Much to Elise's relief, the large man did not advance further. He let out a long, rough sigh and shuffled past Dr. Grout out the door into the approaching evening.

"Good night, folks. I'll be seeing you again soon." And with that Dr. Grout gathered his great girth and toddled out the door.

CHAPTER THREE

The Face in the Tree

Ms. Hopper wilted into a chair, and Mr. Hernandez stood nearby, attempting to catch his breath. Elise's relief did not last long as she glanced over at Ms. Hopper. For once, she looked every bit of her eighty-plus years.

"That tears it," Mr. Hernandez said, smashing his hands together. "He has no right to bring that goon in here to try and intimidate you. You have to refuse him service from now on."

"I-I-I . . . " Ms. Hopper stammered, putting her face into her hands.

"Ms. Hopper, are you OK?" Elise felt her throat tightening.

"I . . . " Ms. Hopper looked up and straightened in her chair. "Yes, I'm fine. I'm closing now."

"But—" Elise blurted.

"No, Elise. I'll be fine." Ms. Hopper glanced at Mr. Hernandez, her hair tower tilting dangerously in the other direction. "Mr. Hernandez is always out and about. If I need anything, I'll reach out to him. I just need to be alone for a while."

"You can't let that Dr. Grout or that James in here anymore," Elise pleaded.

"Sadly, I agree," Ms. Hopper said. "Lynn and I always opened our doors to everyone. I hate to see that change here at the end."

"Is it?" Elise asked, her voice rising.

"Is it what, dear?"

"The end?"

"Well," Ms. Hopper said, "it might be. I can barely remember the recipes, I can't find my Cookbook, and now this. Heebie jeebies."

That Cookbook again! "Can't you get another one?" Elise asked.

"No, sweetie, we've talked about this. It was a special book. It was full of recipes gathered from the witches and fairy folk, not to mention bewitchments, spells, and other hard-gathered knowledge. It can't be replaced."

Elise tried to hold her tongue but saw that Mr. Hernandez was as frustrated by the answer as she was.

"Ms. Hopper, please—enough with the witches and goblins and everything. You could lose your shop!" she nearly shouted.

Ms. Hopper shrank back, her eyes wide, then sighed. "I'm closing early for the evening. I'll see you both tomorrow."

Outside the shop, the sky was beginning to darken. Elise held off the chill by wrapping her arms around herself.

"It's a hard world," Mr. Hernandez said.

Elise huffed. "More like it's a cruel world."

Mr. Hernandez jingled the keys hanging from his belt. His eyebrows went up and down.

"What if . . . " He rubbed at his chin. "What if we got the word out somehow that The Rip Van Winkle Bakery was making world-class desserts again? Then people would come back, wouldn't they?"

"They might, but how are we going to do that?"

"I have an idea," he said, continuing to rub his chin, deep in thought.

"Yes?" Elise prodded.

"Well, my nephew works for the Ichabod Times newspaper."

"And?" Why wouldn't he get to the point?

"Well, he knows the food and art critic. What if we had him come over and review the place? I mean, he comes and tries some of Ms. Hopper's pastries and whatnot? He'll write a good review, and bang, she's back on top of the world." He stood jiggling his keys and smiling at his clever plan.

Elise looked at him doubtfully. "A year ago, maybe, but you see how it is now. She has good days and not-so-good days. What if the critic comes by on a not-so-good day?"

"Well, we see to it that she has a good day. We pitch in and do what we can to help."

"I just wish we could find the Cookbook." Elise shoved her hands into her pockets. "I don't believe that it belonged to Washington Irving or was magical or anything like that, but Ms. Hopper believes it, and if she had the book, maybe she could save the bakery and herself."

Now it was Mr. Hernandez's turn to look doubtful. "I'm sorry to say this, but I don't think she's going to find her lost book anytime soon, sweetie. By the time she figures out where she's misplaced it, it'll be too late. No, I think the best thing to do would be to help her come up with some new recipes and help out with preparing for the critic's visit."

"I don't know." Elise shook her head.

"What else are we going to do?" Mr. Hernandez spread his hands out as if another idea might drop out of the sky and land in them.

"Yeah." Elise sighed. "Well, let's think about it."

"Just an idea, anyway," Mr. Hernandez said while continuing to jingle away. "I'll talk to my nephew about setting up the review."

"OK. Either way, thanks for caring about her, Mr. Hernandez."

"Of course, honey."

❧

Mr. Hernandez's idea bounced around Elise's head as she walked home. Could it work? What if the review turned out to be terrible? Without the Cookbook, it just seemed like a disaster waiting to happen. Maybe she could find another pastry cookbook at the library.

She shivered as the wind began to blow harder. She decided to put the whole thing out of her mind until tomorrow and just hurry home.

As she passed under a row of ancient sycamore trees lining the street, they swayed deeply in the breeze. A low branch brushed the top of her head. She shook herself free and pawed her hair back into place, taking in the earthy but sweet smell of its leaves.

Despite the pleasant scent, she had never liked the row of trees nor the legends of witches once being hung from their high branches or the ones claiming that the trees marked the spot where a rival tribesman had murdered an ancient Indian wizard. Their gnarled knees and scarred trunks seemed like reminders of the horrible things they had seen all those years ago.

Elise tried to ignore these thoughts as she passed the trees on her daily walk to school and back home after work. Often she kept silent as she went by. It was silly, she knew, but they always gave her the strange impression that they were eavesdropping. If only Coop was with her tonight. But then again, who was she kidding? He would have probably just kept his nose in a book, oblivious to her and the spooky trees.

She was nearly past the gauntlet of trees when something caught her eye. At the end of the row, lines were cut about head high into the bark of the last tree. The lines formed a rough circle about the size of a basketball. Sap oozed in glistening droplets from the fresh cuts.

What on earth . . . ? She had no idea what the cuts meant, but they sure added to the trees' creep factor.

She hurried on and was only too happy to reach her house at the corner of Park and Lawrence streets. It was an older structure, prone to odd and creaky noises, but it was home. In the kitchen, her mom, in her white nurse's uniform, was quickly laying out dinner.

"Night shift tonight and running late, love you." Elise's mother said, putting down two glasses of milk. "Tuck yourselves in at a reasonable hour, please." She blew a kiss and headed out through the screened-in front porch.

"Mom—" Elise called, but the porch door banged shut. If only she could talk to her about what was happening to Ms. Hopper and the bakery. But since her dad had disappeared, money had become tight. Her mom had to pick up whatever nursing shifts came open at the hospital, and tonight was no different.

Elise sat down and stared at the sandwich on her plate but couldn't eat. Guilt kept punching at her insides for the way she had snapped at Ms. Hopper.

"What's bugging you?" Stephen mumbled around a mouthful of food.

"What?" Elise looked up at her brother, who blinked at her through his thick, black-rimmed glasses, devouring his sandwich as if he was in a race. "Oh, nothing." How did he stay so rail thin, wolfing his food the way he did?

"Is it your boyfriend?"

Elise scowled. "I don't have a boyfriend."

"But you wish you did." Stephen smirked. "Coop."

"Stop being annoying," Elise snapped.

"Oh, chill out. Anyway, I saw him again this afternoon. He was playing D&D with our crew over at Black's Hardware. We killed a whole troop of orcs. I think he married a fairy princess or something. He didn't mention you." Stephen smirked again.

He finished his sandwich and left his dirty plate on the table. He walked over to the living room, picked up his violin, and began practicing.

"Do you have to do that right now?" Elise shouted over the screeching.

"I do if I want to make orchestra."

Elise squeezed her eyes shut at a particularly shrill note. For someone as smart as Stephen, he sure didn't have much talent for music. He could memorize the notes, just like he could memorize most anything, but that didn't mean he could play.

Their father had had the same gift for memorization, retaining endless facts about early American literature and any other useless trivia he came across. Usually, Stephen's annoying behavior got a pass since their father had disappeared. He looked so much like him and all, but it was just too much tonight.

Elise needed air. She needed to be away from the squawking violin. She needed to apologize to Ms. Hopper. She grabbed her coat. "I'll be back later."

Stephen just nodded and kept scraping at the violin strings.

❧

Outside the winds had redoubled their efforts, and Elise shivered. Should she go back in? No—then she might not get the chance to apologize to Ms. Hopper.

The moon hid behind a thick layer of clouds, and the night was pitch black beyond the pale glow of streetlights. The smell of burning leaf piles from earlier in the day still hung in the air despite the wind. It was a smell that usually made her feel warm inside but not tonight. Halloween decorations flapped and fluttered, and as she approached the dreaded row of sycamores, their branches danced wildly in the wind.

Hunched down into her coat, Elise glanced at the first

tree where she had seen the cuts earlier and stopped as they came into focus. The random lines were no longer random. Someone had added deeper carvings. From the darkness, a twisted face with angled eyes and a long nose was taking shape where the rough circle had been before.

Elise stifled a scream and ran the last block to the bakery. The witches hanging from the lampposts and vampires and mummies lining the streets didn't look funny anymore as she sped past them, panic squeezing her stomach.

When she finally reached the shop, she took several deep breaths. Calm down. There's nothing to be scared of. More composed now, Elise made sure not to step on the string Ms. Hopper always laid out at night across the last step to keep out "trolls and such." She raised her hand to knock on the glass door but stopped short, frozen, her breath floating before her.

Behind the display counters inside, trays moved about in the air. Elise squinted. How . . ? A mop dabbed the floor all by itself, and farther back in the kitchen, she could swear she saw spoons stirring in bowls while eggs cracked themselves and poured out their contents.

Once she remembered to breathe again, Elise inhaled deeply. No. Way. She was almost home before she even realized she was running again.

She didn't slow down for the fluttering witches. She didn't slow down for the swaying sycamore trees, and she especially did not slow down for the terrifying face. She stormed through the front door of the house and only stopped once she was under the safety of the comforter covering her bed.

CHAPTER FOUR

Legends

From the journal of Niles Folsom, High Doctor, October Society of
New York City

Tuesday, October 27, 1986, Legend Hollow, New York

*A*n October Society courier has relayed to me with the utmost
urgency that Ms. Hopper of the Ember Coven has reported
*a sighting of a troll in broad daylight. What's more, the sighting
occurred in her bakery, which doubles as her dwelling.*

*A troll that does not turn to rock in the light of day means only
one thing: it is under the protection of a spell. This type of spell is
rare and thought to be documented in only a few places (and for
good reason, I might add), and one of those is the Cookbook of
Washington Irving and Lana Holland. The troll was seen in the
company of one Dr. Grout. It can only be assumed that the book*

has come into his possession by nefarious means.

I have instructed the members of the October Society, especially the Plumber, the shamans, and the witches' covens, to be on high alert, find the book, and report back any other disturbing developments. Furthermore, they have been instructed to take any action they see fit to protect the citizens of Legend Hollow from spooks going bump in the night or malevolent creatures now stalking us in the light.

Elise sat in math class, staring at the sheet of problems on her desk. She couldn't push the events from the night before from her mind. Math had no chance this morning.

The radiators along the wall of the classroom clinked to life, pushing heat into the room. They were old but comforting.

The other kids in nearby rows worked away on their ditto sheets, oblivious to the thoughts weighing upon her. They weren't concerned with missing fathers, bakeries closing down, or dishes floating through the air. For everyone else, thoughts of costumes and Halloween parties were probably the only things competing with the math lesson. Everyone except Jimmy Manx, that was.

Elise glanced at the large boy. His back was turned to her, his mullet ending in a skinny rat tail, but his mind appeared elsewhere as well. He had been held back twice already and was on the same track this year. Elise would feel sorry for him, but he had been nothing but mean when her dad had disappeared.

"Disappeared? Try he left or he's dead," he had sneered when the subject had come up at school. The other kids had expressed concern for her or said nothing at all, but not Jimmy Manx. He never missed an opportunity to be cruel.

The images of the police in her kitchen popped into her mind. She remembered thinking that nothing had been wrong with her parents or their relationship when Dad had suddenly gone missing. They had seemed so perfect. Her heart ached to think of her mom still looking for him even when the police had given up.

Elise deliberately turned her thoughts away from Jimmy and her dad and checked to see what Coop was doing instead. He, of course, was diligently working on his math page. He had seen the grotesque face in the tree this morning on their walk to school and had just shrugged when Elise asked for his thoughts.

"It looks like a false face mask," he said before going back to his book.

"A what?" Stephen asked.

"Yeah, a what?" Elise asked as well, keeping her eyes on the strange carving as they passed.

"It's an Iroquois tradition. "

"Oh. Well, thanks, that explains a lot," Stephen said rolling his eyes.

Coop let out a long sigh and tucked his book under his arm. "My ancestors and some Iroquois today carve false faces or masks into living trees. Once the mask dries, they cut it from the tree and wear it for rituals or festivals when they dance. Not many people know the tradition these days, though."

"They look freaky," Stephen said, his violin case bumping on the ground behind him.

"Stephen, pick up your violin," Elise admonished her little brother. "So, what's the purpose of the masks?"

"Well, it would depend on the group. No, that's not the

right word. The society—yeah that's it.

"OK." Elise prodded him to continue.

"More?"

"Yes. more! You're kind of leaving us hanging here."

"Well, according to books I've read on the subject, different societies within the Iroquois would wear them for different reasons. For example, the Medicine Society would wear them to cure disease and chase away the spirits that brought illness, or the Husk Society would wear them to humor the spirits that controlled nature."

"Kind of sounds like Halloween," Stephen said.

"I guess," Coop responded.

Spirits? "What about evil or bad spirits?" Elise asked, happy to be at the end of the block and away from the trees and the grotesque mask.

"What about them?" Coop asked.

"Well, do any of the masks keep evil spirits away?"

"Sure, I would think so. The false faces represent the grandfathers of the Iroquois. They're supposed to reconnect humans and nature, giving them the power to frighten the spirits away—well, the bad spirits, anyway. Most of the masks are for that purpose, I guess."

"So, then, the mask we saw probably wasn't meant to scare us. It was meant to scare away bad spirits or something?" Elise asked slowly.

"Sure, I guess so." Coop had glanced at Elise with what she could have sworn was a look of approval. "George First probably did it in anticipation of the fall festival or something." Coop had raised his book back to his face. "He's just weird enough to carve one right here in the middle of town and freak everyone out."

The ringing of the school bell for lunch hour yanked Elise from her thoughts. The aroma of pigs in a blanket and sloppy joes competed with the smell of chalkboard erasers, ditto sheets, and dried glue accumulated over the years. She packed up her blank math sheet and resigned herself to having extra homework tonight.

"Hey, walk with you to the cafeteria?" Coop said, sliding through the torrent of exiting kids.

"Not today."

"Oh. OK then." Coop sounded a little hurt.

"I didn't mean it that way. I meant I'm eating my lunch in the library today." She slung her backpack over her shoulder. "You can come if you want. I've got some research to do."

"Sure, I guess." He pulled a book from his backpack and opened it in front of his face as they headed upstairs.

The steps were so old that grooves had been worn in the edges from generations of students placing their feet in the same spots. At the top, they turned left and headed for the library, passing through the ancient gymnasium where some kids were tossing and dribbling basketballs. The floorboards rose and fell like small waves in a brown lake. Halloween decorations hung from the high rafters. Black cats and pumpkins swayed gently above them as Elise and Coop passed below.

Some of the pumpkins had been turned upside down near the high windows, and some were even shredded. A couple of jars hung from strings with unidentifiable items in them. Strange. What kid could even climb up that high?

Elise nudged Coop. "Hey, put that away for a second."

"Sure." Coop lowered his book.

"That face in the tree got me wondering."

"About what?" Coop asked as they entered another short hallway.

"You know how you said Native Americans carve masks to keep spirits away?"

"Some spirits."

"Well, what do you know about these—creatures?" Elise asked. "You know, like kobolds, fairies, trolls, and that stuff?"

"Oh, I thought you were talking about Native American legends. Sounds like you meant D&D." Coop stopped walking. "So, like kobolds, for example, they usually have an armor class of seven, and live in cave networks—"

"D&D dorks!" a voice boomed from behind them.

Jimmy Manx. "Shut up," Elise hissed. The warmth of embarrassment spread through her body like a fever. Coop slid his book back in front of his face, ignoring the bully.

"What are you little wizards going to do? You gonna turn me into a frog or something?" Jimmy grinned, showing yellowed teeth.

"Trust me, if I could I would have already," said Elise. "Anyway, mind your own business."

"Yeah," Coop said quietly from behind his book.

Jimmy lunged at Coop, who flinched behind the book, then pulled back. "Ha! You ain't worth it, redskin." Apparently satisfied, Jimmy pushed past the two of them.

"I hate that guy," Coop said once Jimmy was gone.

"Yeah." Elise started walking again, and Coop fell in beside her. "Anyway," she said, lowering her voice, "I guess I meant more like real-life stories of monsters." Elise's face immediately felt hot again as she looked around to make sure no other kids had heard the comment.

"Real life?" Coop raised an eyebrow and shot Elise a

sideways look. "That mask must have really gotten to you."

"No, I don't mean in real life. Geez! I guess the mask got my mind wandering a little." Her face felt even hotter, if that was possible.

"OK."

They reached the library, a double-sized room still not nearly big enough for the number of books that it contained. Stacks upon stacks of books lined shelves that climbed toward the ceiling. Kids referred to the room as "the belly of the beast"—not because of the piles of books but because of the noises often coming from beneath its floor.

The school's ancient boiler room lay directly below with the boilers working day and night to sustain the heat and hot water for the large school. Sam, the rarely seen but often heard maintenance man, fought to keep the boilers running. He was a small, thin man always dressed in blue overalls and perpetually unshaven. When the boilers began to groan and moan under the strain of their work, Sam could often be heard shouting encouragement.

When the boilers failed, as they often did, the sounds of Sam clanking on the machines with his tools and muttering curses about "gremlins and goblins" seeped through the library floor. This delighted the kids, who dutifully read in silence, allowing Sam's bad language to spread through the library much to the librarian's dismay.

The boiler room itself was an area few students had ever seen firsthand. Rumors abounded of horrible dangers and secrets contained behind its locked door. Elise had often heard classmates conjure the tallest of tails only limited by the heights of their imagination. Case in point: a door in the boiler room floor supposedly led to a haunted basement where misbehaving students were sent to ponder their actions in the dark.

Of course, Elise didn't believe the punishment part—no way the school could get away with that!—but the haunted part did catch her attention. She had asked her dad about the rumor, and he had said that the school had been built on the site of an eighteenth-century graveyard belonging to early Dutch settlers. The graveyard had been relocated before the school was built, but maybe not all of the remains had been found and moved.

Elise grabbed a reading table in the middle of the room, and they unpacked their sack lunches.

"So," Elise continued after a couple of minutes of munching, "if you did see some of these Iroquois spirits in person, the ones the masked people were trying to drive away, what would they look like?" She wasn't sure rewording her question made it sound any less crazy. She swallowed a bite of her sandwich and pushed on.

"I mean, would they be little people? Would they appear as creatures with monster heads or no heads at all or like something else? I mean, what are we talking about?"

"You realize I've never seen one, right?" Coop put his own sandwich down. Elise felt herself turn red again, and she could tell it didn't escape his attention.

"All stories or, you know, oral traditions start somewhere, right?" Coop said. "I guess some people just come up with them in their imagination, and some are based on some sort of truth no matter how small it might be. Even stories people imagine or come up with have to come from somewhere. They say that there's a kernel of truth to every fairy tale."

"Wow, you should be a teacher instead of a student," Elise

said with a laugh.

"Like your dad?"

Elise inhaled sharply, and Coop realized his mistake immediately.

"Elise, I'm sorry."

"No, it's OK." She managed a weak smile. "I know you didn't mean anything. He used to say some of the same things. He said Washington Irving's tales were just explanations of the unknown for early Americans. Entertain them with their own fears. He said back then they were living out in the wilderness, right? They needed to have the unexplained explained. It was a way for them to have their fears brought out of the darkness and into the light." She could hear his voice when speaking the words.

Coop grabbed his D&D Monster Manual from his backpack and began flipping through pages, pointing out samples of magic folk from pixies to elves.

"These were all probably based on some creature people saw out in the wilds and didn't understand or some strange natural phenomena, so they made up legends and stories about them."

"Can any of them turn invisible?" Elise tried to chew her sandwich casually.

Coop raised both eyebrows. "Well, I suppose pixies or sprites could." He pointed to a page with a drawing of a winged faerie sitting on a mushroom. "Invisibility would be one of their special abilities, it says here. They have good saving roles versus magic attacks as well, in case you were wondering."

"What about something called kobolds?" Ms. Hopper often used that word. Sometimes she called them dwarfs or friends who "helped out around the bakery."

Coop had stopped bothering with the strange looks and dutifully turned to a page with pictures of kobolds.

"Nasty little dog-like humanoid creatures. Pure evil. I slayed a band of twenty of them one time. Orlem, my magic user, used a fireball spell." Coop smiled with pride.

"But these don't look or sound anything like what I would have expected or how she described them."

"Described? By who?" Coop looked puzzled.

"Um—just something I saw on TV." Elise continued to frown down at the page. Should she ask about dwarfs? Maybe she'd pushed it too far already. She didn't want Coop to think she was even weirder than he probably already thought she was.

"You know, maybe you need to come to game night," Coop said. "Your brother will be there. All of this would be much clearer after playing a couple of campaigns."

"Sure, maybe." The invitation made Elise's stomach turn sour. They were in eighth grade now. Was he really asking a girl to sit around a table with a bunch of boys and play dice games all night?

She tried to stuff her frustrations away. After all, Coop had stuck by her in the year since her father had disappeared, and for that alone she was grateful. People had talked, whispering that her father had abandoned her family or gone off into the woods and gone crazy. The rumors had hurt, and she'd withdrawn to keep her distance from them.

They hadn't talked much about what had happened, and Elise was fine with that. Coop had been there for her, and that was what mattered. His parents had divorced years before, and he seemed somehow to understand the pain she was going through.

"I'll be right back." Elise shoved her chair away from the table. "I'm going to see what books they have on mythology and stuff. I need it for a writing assignment in English class."

"OK," Coop said, sliding his Monster Manual back into his backpack.

The card catalog was not helpful. It had mostly books on Greek mythology and Christmas elves, garden gnomes and other similar stuff. Why didn't they have anything on local legends? Elise wandered the shelves but found nothing on kobolds, just some D&D and Hobbit books and kiddy stuff with silly drawings. She wasn't even sure what she was looking for. She headed back to Coop.

"This is a big zero for me. I think I'm going to head to the city library tonight." She paused. "Um—do you want to go with me?"

"I can, but not until around seven o'clock. Tonight is D&D game night at Black's Hardware, remember?"

"Right. So, you'll go with me?"

"Sure."

Elise grinned as the boilers groaned to life beneath their feet, and Sam the maintenance man could be heard shouting his support.

CHAPTER FIVE

Spirits, Goblins, and Trolls

Elise could swear that her heart was beating thousands of times a minute as she approached the bakery after school. Inside, she found that all of the worrying had been unnecessary. Ms. Hopper was behind the counter, filling display trays. A few customers straggled in and out, but nothing seemed out of the ordinary. It was just a regular afternoon.

"Hello, Elise. I saved you a Covered Bridge Coffee Cake. It has crumbled brown sugar and maple spice on top. It was the best seller of the day."

"Thanks, Ms. Hopper." She stowed away her backpack. "Ms. Hopper?"

"Yes, sweetie."

"I'm really sorry about snapping at you yesterday."

"Oh, silly billy, I know you are." Ms. Hopper reached out

and patted Elise's shoulder. "We've been under some strain with the way things have been going lately. Everyone's a little on edge, so don't you worry about it."

Elise's shoulders relaxed. "Thank you, Ms. Hopper."

"Of course."

"Um, did Dr. Grout and that man come back today?"

"No, sweetie, they didn't. Now try your coffee cake." Ms. Hopper pushed the dessert toward Elise.

Elise took a bite. It was much better than yesterday's treat, which gave her hope.

"Good?" Ms. Hopper asked, looking doubtful.

"Delish, Ms. Hopper."

"That's good news, considering . . . "

"Considering what?" Elise pushed the cake to the side.

"Well, Mr. Martinez was able to talk to his son at the newspaper, and . . . "

"And?" Elise asked.

"Wham, bam, bang, his son was able to convince the restaurant critic to come into the shop to do a review two days after Halloween!" Ms. Hopper clapped her hands together.

"Oh," Elise said, surprised. Just six days from now. Her stomach squeezed.

"Just oh?" Ms. Hopper's smile vanished.

"No, I mean, that's good news." She paused. "But that means we need to be at our best."

"Well, of course." Ms. Hopper nodded, the Leaning tower of Pisa swaying back and forth on top of her head.

"I mean, well, it's Wednesday now, and Halloween is this weekend. We need to start coming up with some of your best recipes right away if we're going to impress this critic."

"I know, sweetie, I know." Ms. Hopper let out a long sigh.

"Heckity sheckity, if I could just find that Cookbook."

"Maybe if you could remember some of your recipes, you could write them down," Elise suggested. "Even if it's just parts of them, and then we can try and fill in the blanks."

"I can try" Ms. Hopper rubbed her forehead as if that might make the memories come back.

Later, after Elise had finished her sweeping, she sat down next to Ms. Hopper as she totaled up the receipts.

"Ms. Hopper, you know how you put the string across the door at night?"

"Yes, to keep out spirits, goblins, and trolls," Ms. Hopper said absently.

"Yes, that. Have you ever actually seen any spirits, goblins, or trolls?"

"Well, that's an odd question. Have you seen any spirits, goblins, or trolls lately?" Her bright eyes were inquisitive.

"No. But you have, right?" Elise asked.

"Yes, a few."

"How did you know to put out the string? How did you know about the trolls and kobolds and stuff?"

"Interesting questions." Ms. Hopper continued to gaze at Elise thoughtfully.

Elise squirmed. "I'm just saying, I don't see these things you talk about, but you seem so convinced."

"Hmm," Ms. Hopper said. "I get that." She began gathering her receipts into a single pile. "When we have more time, we can have a longer discussion to answer your questions."

"No, Ms. Hopper." Elise's heart thumped. "I need to talk about it now."

"Oh." Ms. Hopper seemed taken aback. "Well, sure, if it's so important to you, we can talk now." She put the receipts aside. "Where to begin . . . "

"Are you saying that monsters are running about everywhere? Do you mean it when you claim 'kobolds' help you in the bakery?" Elise made air quotes with her fingers and then crossed her arms. She didn't mean to be defiant, but she really needed to be convinced?

"Kobolds?" Ms. Hopper repeated the word, smiling. "I don't necessarily see 'monsters,' but things like trolls, goblins, spirits—they're part of our story."

"Like, they existed in the past?" Elise asked.

"Yes, but they still exist today. Zoom, boom, maybe they're here in the room." Ms. Hopper's eyes went wide as she looked over both of her shoulders and then laughed.

Impatience bubbled up inside Elise. "OK, jokes aside, I've seen you put string across your doorway, but I've never seen what it's supposed to be stopping."

"Then it must be working. I put the string across my doorway for things I don't want to see."

"Why do you think something so silly—" Elise caught herself. "I mean, how do you know something like putting a string down will work?"

"It's the sort of knowledge has been passed down from person to person," Ms. Hopper responded. "Folks have been doing it in the old country and out in the hollows for generations to keep out those meanie weenies. You don't want uninvited guests entering your home, do you?"

"So, you hear the stories and legends, and you just take them as the absolute truth?" Elise looked blankly at Ms. Hopper.

"Legends and stories come from somewhere, don't they? They're based on some truth somewhere, no matter how small, right?"

Elise stared. That's the second time I've heard that today. "So, all the scary stories are true, then?"

"No, sweetie, I'm not saying that." Ms. Hopper tried again. "OK, for example, what are we celebrating this weekend?"

"Halloween?"

"Right—Halloween or All Hallows Eve, as some of us call it. What are some of the fun traditions you're doing to celebrate Halloween?"

"Um, I don't know—I guess dress up and carve a pumpkin. Maybe watch the Peanuts Halloween special." What was Ms. Hopper getting at?

"OK, so Halloween started somewhere, right?"

"Yes, I guess," Elise answered.

"In fact, it began as a festival in old-country Europe among the Celts and other people. They called it Samhain." The word rolled off her tongue: sah-win. "Why?" she asked, then immediately answered her own question. "At the end of summer, these people feared that the barrier between our world and the world of ghosts and evil spirits was at its thinnest. Particularly on the evening of October 31st." Ms. Hopper's eyes widened.

"They would have a big party, lighting bonfires and donning costumes to scare the bad spirits back to their world. When European immigrants came to America, they brought the holiday with them, and it evolved into Halloween with its tricks and treats, give me sweets, and the rest."

"Including pumpkins?" Elise asked.

"Zippity bippity, that's another good example!" She seemed pleased with Elise's comprehension. "A pumpkin is just a gourd, right? The fruit of the pumpkin vine, if you will." Ms. Hopper made a round gesture with her hands.

"Sure." Elise shrugged.

"Nothing special, right?" The hair pile on top of Ms. Hopper's head leaned sharply to the left.

"I guess not."

"So, why do we carve them?" The hair tilted in the other direction.

"I don't know. For fun? The holiday?" Frustration rose in Elise's chest.

"Maybe, but why did we start carving them? Why has this tradition been passed down from generation to generation?" Ms. Hopper did not wait for Elise to answer. "It started with the Irish. They carved gourds with faces. They did it to keep the bad spirits and goblins away and to protect their harvest. When they came to America, they continued the tradition, but instead of gourds, they began carving pumpkins because that's what they found growing here."

"Oh," Elise said.

"These traditions, these stories, are based on things that people see and can't explain or things they don't understand or just plain come out of fear and wanting to protect themselves. The stories are meant to explain those things or at least give shape to the mysterious and confront their fears of the unknown or unexplained. But these tales are not simply made up out of whole cloth, of course. As I said, they spring from small truths, knowledge gained and lessons learned over time. Look at Legend Hollow." Ms. Hopper spread her hands around in a large circle above her head. "We're famous for Washington Irving, and what was he famous for?"

"For his stories? For entertaining us?" Elise answered.

"Yes, sweetie beatie, he did entertain us, but he also

passed on the legends and knowledge that he had gathered from the people of the hollows and the mountains. He spoke with the descendants of the early settlers, gathered the stories of the freed African slaves, and collected the legends of the original Native Americans. He gathered it all and passed on their knowledge. This is why your father thought his stories were so important. Mr. Irving gave us a road map to the unexplained and unlocked our fears when he told us stories of headless horsemen or mischievous spirits bringing poor Rip Van Winkle to grief by making him sleep all those years. Jiminy biminy, there were lessons for us all in those tales." Ms. Hopper's gaze seemed far off.

"Is that why he wrote the Cookbook, then?" Elise asked, trying to bring Ms. Hopper back from wherever her mind had gone.

"Well, yes and no. That was a little different," she said with a slight smile. "He was putting that together to impress my great-great-great-aunt Lana, a renowned baker and lover of sweets, among other things. When he met with people to gather lore, often he was just as vigorously gathering enchanted recipes."

"Odd," Elise said under her breath.

"Not so odd, you little noddy toddy," Ms. Hopper said, her eyes twinkling. "You'll see someday when you're in love. Mr. Irving would have done just about anything to secure the affection of Miss Holland. She was his paramour."

Elise wrinkled her brow. "Paramour?"

"A girlfriend, if you will. Mr. Irving had a significant other, but when he came to Legend Hollow researching his books and gathering stories, he met Aunt Holland, and they carried on quite a romance from what I understand." Ms. Hopper's face pinkened.

"But people say Washington Irving never came to Legend Hollow," Elise protested. "That it's just a rumor that the town's Chamber of Commerce made up to drum up tourism."

"Your father's research indicated that he visited multiple times." Ms. Hopper gave Elise a sharp look.

"I know, but people say . . . "

"Well, either way, the reason that his visits were kept hush-hush was that he did not want his significant other to find out."

"I see." Elise wasn't sure she saw.

"The Cookbook was an attempt to secure Lana's love. She accepted the book and through the years recorded her own spells and enchantments in it, expanding it well beyond the special recipes it originally contained. She was the librarian, if you will, of the Ember Coven of witches, and in that same book, she recorded the coven's collected knowledge of the natural, the unnatural, and the spirit world. The Cookbook became a very powerful tome, as you can imagine. It's a bit of a disaster to lose it, really." Ms. Hopper's voice trailed off and she began to look weary.

"I . . . " Elise tried to absorb all of this, but she was still skeptical. Was she getting tricked by an old lady having fun at her expense? Or maybe Ms. Hopper had simply lost touch with reality. "OK, magic cookbooks aside, let's go back. Let's talk about the spirits, the unexplained, the creatures that you say are at the root of these legends."

"Yes?" Ms. Hopper seemed to regain her strength.

"Can some of them make things float?"

"Float?" Ms. Hopper asked, her eyebrows rising.

"Maybe mixing things in bowls, moving brooms?" The

image of the busy bakery from the other night swam through Elise's mind.

"That is . . . very specific." Ms. Hopper now looked slightly alarmed. But before she could continue, a crash came from the kitchen.

"What was that?" Elise exclaimed, jumping from her chair.

"Oh, nibbly bibbly—time to go, sweetie," Ms. Hopper said without turning toward the commotion. "You head on home. I'll deal with this."

TAYLOR PENSONEAU

CHAPTER SIX

Hardware Stores and Dungeon Masters

Elise did not go home. Instead, she walked six blocks to downtown where Black's Hardware was located. Once inside, she passed through the garden section, rows of flooring materials, and power tools finally stopping near the back of the building. There several people, including Coop and her little brother, Stephen, sat around a card table playing a rowdy game of D&D.

Oddly enough, Black's Hardware had been the first place in Legend Hollow where kids could buy D&D books and supplies. Bill Black, whose family owned the hardware store and who served as the dungeon master, sat at the head of the table, wearing a purple wizard's hat. Elise had always thought the hat bordered on goofy for somebody in their mid-twenties, but Bill wore it all the time—when working at the shop, hanging out at the mall, or even walking around town.

Bill's obsession with the game had dismayed his family, but it ended up benefitting the business to no end. Legions of adolescent boys insisted on going to the hardware store every week to look at the D&D manuals, rule books, modules and talk about the role-playing game, dragging along their parents, who ended up shopping.

Elise looked around at the surrounding shelves. Nails, check. Garden hoses, check. Sandpaper, check. Miniature figures of elves and orcs and twenty-sided dice, check.

"You come to a clearing in the forest and hear the sounds of battle. Your torches do not give off enough light to see the combatants on this moonless night," Bill said from behind his dungeon master's privacy screen. Only his pointed wizard's hat appeared above it.

"My elf readies his sword and runs toward the noise using his infravision," Stephen said, moving a tiny elf figure across what appeared to be a map.

"Caution, Elric my elven friend," Coop said in a falsely deep voice.

Elise giggled. Coop glanced her way.

"Oh, hey, Elise." He showed no signs of embarrassment.

"Hey, Coop." Elise stepped out from behind the shelves.

"I see you accepted my invitation." He looked pleased.

"Of course she did," Stephen said, looking up from his character sheet.

Elise's face warmed. Bill's face rose above his dungeon master screen, looking annoyed.

"Anyway," he said, disappearing back behind the screen. "You're too late, Bruno. Elric charges into the clearing, and his night vision reveals two trolls and several goblins attacking a caravan of human travelers. One of the trolls charges forward and immediately attacks Elric. Roll for initiative."

"Elise, do you want to join in? We have some non-player characters you could use," Coop said, ignoring Bill.

That was all she needed—to get stuck among a bunch of wizards and elves for the next hour. "No, I'm good. You guys go ahead. I'll just do some homework until you're done."

"You seem familiar?" Bill's face popped up again, still annoyed.

"She's my sister," Stephen said, grabbing a twenty-sided die.

"Oh." Bill looked Elise up and down. Without further comment, he ducked back behind his dungeon master's screen. Elise could hear dice rolling before Bill shouted.

"Let's get back to it, gentlemen. We are at battle, and a troll is closing in!"

∽

An hour later Coop and Elise headed for the city library with Stephen tagging along. Stephen knew better than to annoy Elise further with the boyfriend jokes and was quiet on the short walk.

The library was a two-story brick structure built in the 1950s during Legend Hollow's better times. A short, wide stairway led to double doors made of glass and copper. Inside, Elise and the others found themselves on the first floor near two librarian desks.

There were few patrons in the building at this late hour, and only one librarian was working. She was an older woman with white hair, wearing a blue wool dress and reading a dog-eared paperback paying them little attention.

The first floor was mostly card catalogs, study tables, a children's section, and magazine shelves. The card catalog was Elise's first stop. She still wasn't sure how much to tell Coop about what she was looking for.

"Still focusing on mythological creatures for that research paper?" Coop asked.

"I think so." Elise kept it cool. "You know, like we were discussing earlier. Like how they appear in stories and stuff. Maybe something about their origins and history."

"Did I hear research paper?" Stephen asked from behind them.

"Yes," Elise answered.

"No, thank you. I'm heading over to the magazine section. Going to see what's new this month in video games."

That was no surprise. When he wasn't practicing the violin or playing D&D, he could reliably be found at Aladdin's Castle, the arcade at the mall.

"OK, we'll swing by and find you on the way out. We'll probably be upstairs in a bit."

"OK." Stephen ran off around the corner.

Coop was already rifling through the card catalog and scribbling numbers on scratch paper. Elise peeked over his shoulder to see what he had written.

"I thought since we struck out with my Monster Manual, we would try any books dealing with mythology."

"That sounds like a plan."

The two compiled a list of nearly a dozen books and headed for the second-floor stairs. Two brass statues adorned the posts on the railings. On the left was a bust of Shakespeare, and on the right was a statute of a small man with a long nose. He wore loose-fitting, old-fashioned clothing. In his teeth, he gripped a long, thin pipe, and with his right hand, he extended a mug toward passersby.

Elise had seen the statute a dozen times but had never paid it much attention, just chalking it up to more Washington Irving stuff. This time she stopped and examined him closer. For the first time, she noticed an inscription at the base of the statue. Bending down, she read a fateful drink offered from a tiny hand. from washington irving's rip van winkle.

It was now Coop's turn to look over Elise's shoulder.

"One of the dwarfs or spirits from the Rip Van Winkle story, I believe," he said. "You know—like the story the bakery is named after."

"Also known as a kobold?" Elise asked, still staring.

"Yeah, I guess I hadn't thought of that. Dwarfs or little guys like this are sometimes referred to as kobolds. Can't remember if this guy was supposed to be a dwarf or a ghost."

The hairs on Elise's neck rose as she turned and headed back for the card catalog. "Maybe we need to grab some books on Washington Irving as well."

⌀

Twenty minutes later, they had gathered over a dozen books. They clomped upstairs, struggling under the heavy loads.

They found a large table and chairs tucked between tall shelves of hardback books organized by number. Elise inhaled the musty smell of the old books deeply. Ah, the smell of knowledge!

She started with books about Washington Irving's most famous stories. She zeroed in on one which offered scholarly research on The Legend of Sleepy Hollow and Rip Van Winkle and a couple of others. Scanning the table of contents, she looked for anything mentioning kobolds or little people like the statue. It didn't take long to find references to both in her research of Rip Van Winkle.

Elise scribbled on her pad of paper. The author indicated that the little people who lured Rip Van Winkle into his long snooze were supposed to be ghosts, but their inspiration was described as dwarfs, sometimes goblins, and yes, even kobolds! Elise finished her note and slapped her pencil down.

"Good information?" Coop asked.

"Yes. Let's shrink our search to dwarfs or kobolds but not your D&D kind. More like mischievous little folk like the one on the stairs."

"Will do." Coop gave a salute, smiling, then marched off into the shelves. Elise shook her head.

She turned her attention to a collection of essays about Washington Irving's life. They discussed New York City, Sleepy Hollow, and Tarrytown, but there was no mention of him ever visiting Gould Hollow or Legend Hollow.

Before writing Rip Van Winkle, the researcher said, Irving took trips to the nearby Hudson Valley and even to Europe to gather inspiration from old-country legends and tales for his own stories. The book described how Irving took special interest in the stories originating in what was now called Germany and also Scandinavia, centering around trolls, goblins, dwarfs, and kobolds. We have the next breadcrumb on our trail, Elise thought.

She took more notes as Coop returned. He held books on Snow White and the Seven Dwarfs and the Grimm Brothers in one arm and Native American mythology in the other. As

Coop began reading, Elise went on the hunt for books on German and European mythology.

Upon her return, Coop looked up excitedly. "Here's what I've got so far."

Elise dropped her new stack of books on the table and waited as patiently as she could.

"So, Snow White and The Seven Dwarfs obviously has dwarfs in it, and as I said earlier, dwarfs were often called kobolds in Europe. So, next, we should ask what is the source material for Snow White and the Seven Dwarfs?" Coop grabbed a book from his pile and presented it to Elise.

"It was the Grimm Brothers and their tale Snow White from their collection Grimms' Fairy Tales." Coop pointed to a book sitting to his left. "Many of their tales weren't original, according to the research I just read. Many were existing German, French, and Italian stories they collected from others, even collected from their local library and then presented as their own." Coop looked up, beaming with pride at his digging.

"And?" Elise said, trying to hide her impatience.

"Oh." The smile disappeared from Coop's face, and he continued. "Well, listen to this. It'll make having to go to school every day sound not so bad. The dwarfs in the original Snow White were supposedly based on children who were forced to work in the local copper and iron mines. Their growth was stunted due to the poor conditions, and their limbs were gnarled from the work. That's one theory at least. Another is that those same dwarfs in the story were most likely inspired by old German myths." Coop leaned back again, pleased with his work.

"Very good, professor." Elise grinned at Coop, and he

returned the smile. That was interesting! "And there we are with the German and European myths again," she added, scribbling more notes.

"Again?" Coop asked.

"Washington Irving. I was reading that the small men, the ghosts in Rip Van Winkle, were inspired by dwarfs, goblins, or kobolds of German and Scandinavian myth."

"Good work! I guess we should call you a professor as well." The smile lingered on Coop's face. "So, we have a common thread now with these kobolds in European mythology and folk tales. But let me add another thread. Those same Europeans that immigrated here in the 1600s and 1700s," Coop grabbed a third book from his stack, titled Native American Myth and Legends. "I read here that while many of the European immigrants brought legends and folk tales to America, they weren't the only ones who had such tales. The Native Americans had their own tales of little creatures and people that predated the arrival of the Europeans."

"So, these things have been here a long time. I mean, they've been in folk tales and legends for a long time." Elise corrected herself before Coop could give her one of his looks.

"Yeah." Coop gave her a look anyway before continuing to read his notes. "The Native Americans had something called jogah. I guess they were like little people. They came from Iroquois folk tales. They're dwarf-like nature spirits about two to three feet tall." Coop lowered his hand to about three feet from the ground to illustrate.

"Some called them stone throwers or stone rollers. The book says they're invisible most of the time but sometimes reveal themselves to humans—mostly to children, elders, and medicine people. They might play tricks and even be dangerous to people who disrespect them or their home, but they're generally friendly toward Iroquois and will sometimes do favors for people who leave tobacco or other offerings for them."

"They sound a lot like the European kobolds," Elise said. "Wait a second." She grabbed a book on European mythology and flipped quickly through the pages until she found what she was looking for. "Here—it says that kobolds are often invisible as well."

"Interesting," Coop said, and stood up. "I'm going to pull more books on European legends and myths from the shelves and see what I can find on the invisibility part. You're going to have one heck of a research paper here." He walked around the corner to the next row of shelves.

For a moment, Elise's stomach twinged. Should she tell Coop the real reason they were doing all this research? Not yet. Elise turned to the glossary of her own book on European mythology, looking for kobolds. The glossary said they could be found on page eighty-five. She flipped to that page and began taking notes as quickly as she could write.

Apparently, kobolds were known to help friendly households with things like cooking and cleaning while the families were asleep at night if they were allowed to sleep by a warm fire or keep a portion of what they cooked.

Elise's thoughts turned immediately to the day before and the floating brooms and mixing bowls with their wooden spoons stirring on their own. She thought of Ms. Hopper's frequent claims of assistance from kobolds. Was it really true? A strange feeling prickled the back of her neck, and she looked quickly over her shoulder. Nothing. She shrugged it off.

"Coop, you still over there?" Elise called.

"Yeah?" Coop answered from the other side of the shelves.

"Have you found anything discussing how you can make invisible kobolds not so invisible? I mean, how you can make them visible, like in a house or something they might be in?"

"Um, let me see. I saw one book that said they get angry when humans play petty tricks on them and will leave. But I guess that wasn't what you were asking. Let me keep looking."

Elise heard pages flipping as Coop was silent for a couple of minutes.

"OK," he finally said. "It says here that kobolds rarely appear visible to house inhabitants. Rather, they usually wander about protected by their fog hats, which make them invisible and thus unnoticed. Again, it stresses that one should not make them angry as they can become mean and vicious and do all types of harm to those who offend them."

Elise brushed aside the warning. They were little folk. How much harm could they do? "How do you make them visible?"

"Let me see," Coop said. Before he could continue, a book slid from the shelf near Elise and landed on the floor with a thud.

"Careful," Elise said.

"What?"

"Careful."

"Careful of what?"

"Never mind," Elise said, putting the book back on the shelf. "Just tell me what you found."

"Alright, this might be relevant." She heard pages flip again before he continued. "There's a German folk tale where a baker is always missing some of his loaves of bread when he's done baking each day, but he can never catch the thief. He begins to suspect that it's kobolds, so he waves a basket in a sweeping motion until he knocks the hats off several of them. Without the hats, they can no longer remain invisible."

More page flipping. Then Coop continued.

"Here's another story about someone who suspects she has kobolds and spreads flour on the floor at night and in the morning finds their footprints. When she declares that she knows the creatures are in the house, they became visible. I think—"

Half a dozen books fell from the shelves, crashing to the floor.

"Oh!" Elise exclaimed.

Coop came running around the corner.

"What was that?" His eyes wide.

Elise rubbed at her prickling neck. "That—that wasn't you?"

Before Coop could answer, another row of books came crashing down, narrowly missing them both.

"Let's get out of here!" Coop exclaimed.

Elise didn't hesitate. They quickly gathered their notes and backpacks, left the books on the table, and ran through the second-floor shelves as random books continued to fall around them. What was happening?

Elise ran down the stairs as fast as she dared with Coop following close behind. The librarian dropped her book and stared opened mouthed as they sprinted to the magazine section.

Stephen saw them coming and put his reading back on the rack.

"Geez, is the place on fire?"

"No time—grab my hand," Elise blurted.

More books began to fall. The librarian, who had been

fast walking toward them, wagging her finger and making disapproving sounds, skidded to a stop, eyes unblinking, when she noticed that more books were falling and the children were not the cause. Elise and the others ran past the frozen librarian. The only sounds in the building were their footsteps echoing off the hard floor and the rapid thud of books that continued to tumble to the ground.

Outside, they continued to run until they reached the end of the block.

"What the what . . . ?" Stephen was trying to ask between gasps.

Coop finally began to recover and stood up straight. "Are you OK?" he asked Elise, who was still bent with her hands on her knees, trying to breathe through the exertion and panic.

"I—I think so." She looked over her shoulder toward the library. It seemed quiet and peaceful from this distance.

"Good." Coop took another deep breath and smiled. "That was some first date."

CHAPTER SEVEN

A Kobold Trap

From the journal of Niles Folsom, High Doctor, October Society of
New York City

Wednesday, October 28, 1986, Legend Hollow, New York

*R*eports have reached my desk of a curious incident involving
children vandalizing the Legend Hollow library. Frankly,
the descriptions of books flying from the shelves and librarians
going into hysterics seem more like the work of malcontent
banshees than misbehaving adolescents. A member of the October
Society has been dispatched to investigate the incident further.

Separately, spies among the November Men have reported
that Dr. Grout indeed has the Cookbook and has moved it
underground for safekeeping. It is assumed that this means it
has been taken to the Goblin Market beneath Legend Hollow. A

council of the Legend Hollow October Society will meet tomorrow morning at the Plumber's to discuss recovery plans for the book.

"It's nice to see you so early in the morning," Ms. Hopper said as she placed a tray of pumpkin-iced muffins dusted with candy corn crumbles into the display case.

"My mom had an early nursing shift, and I didn't feel like making anything, so Stephen and I thought we'd stop by on the way to school for breakfast," Elise said, selecting a muffin from the tray.

Stephen sat at a table, already halfway through his second muffin and a glass of milk. Lilah lay on her back at his feet, waiting impatiently for a tummy rub. Her short back legs kicked at Stephen's ankles to remind him that she was there.

An older gentleman sitting at a table next to Stephen laughed at the sight. Ms. Hopper laughed as well.

"Well, you children please eat your fill. The only charge is giving Lilah a good rub-a-dub."

"Will do," Stephen said, cleaning his plate. "The muffins are great this morning." He reached down to scratch Lilah's belly.

"Music to my ears, Stephen. We got the recipe wrong on the first three tries last night." Ms. Hopper's hair tower tilted to the side as she pulled at her earlobe. "It's just so darn hard to remember those recipes."

"Since you finally remembered that recipe, let's get it written down so we can use it again on Tuesday when the critic comes in."

Elise fished her notebook out of her backpack, but she intentionally left her pencil in the pocket. "I can't seem to find a pencil. Do you have an extra one?" she asked, knowing what the answer would be.

"Of course, sweetie," Ms. Hopper said. "There's one on the desk in back."

The front door opened, and Ms. Hopper's friend Ms. Thorstad entered. Her grey purse matched her grey two-piece outfit and grey hat.

"Oh, hello, Ms. Thorstad." Ms. Hopper smiled in welcome.

"I'll get the pencil," Elise said, hurrying past Ms. Hopper and admiring Ms. Thorstad's outfit. She marveled at how she always managed to match her purse and hat with whichever color she had chosen for the day.

"Marge." Ms. Thorstad shuffled to the counter. "What have you got for me today? Something with a little rum in it, perhaps?"

A rare use of Ms. Hopper's first name, Elise noted.

"Oh, no, just Deep Hollow Chocolate Bark this morning. No rum, no wine, or sherry today." Ms. Hopper laughed at their shared joke.

In the back room, Elise grabbed a pencil from the desk Ms. Hopper used to do her paperwork. The spare key to the front door hung from a peg above it. She looked over her shoulder out toward the display cases and customer tables. The doorway was clear. She snatched the spare key and slipped it into her jeans pocket.

"Did you find it, sweetie?" Ms. Hopper hollered from the other room.

"Yes, I'm just going to give it a quick sharpening," Elise called.

She searched hastily among the various ingredient jars holding items like thyme, lavender, dried cloves, almonds, honey, sugar, ginger and cinnamon sticks. There were still others just marked with an X or even a question mark and one labeled with what looked like a picture of a frog.

She brushed past these jars until she found a mixing bowl full of flour. She took a zip-lock plastic bag from a drawer and spooned it nearly full, then stuffed the baggie into another pocket, brushed off her hands, and headed back into the bakery. She was careful not to puncture the bag of flour when she sat down.

"OK, Ms. Hopper, let's write down what you can remember of the recipe for these muffins with candy corn crumbles," Elise said, opening her notebook.

❧

That night Elise told her mom that she was heading over to Coop's house to work on math.

"OK, be home by 9:30," her mom shouted from the kitchen. Outside, Coop paced the sidewalk in front of Elise's house.

"What did you tell your mom?" he asked

"Homework."

"Same here." Coop's eyebrows wrinkled into a frown. He appeared uncomfortable with the false story he had given his mom.

"My mom's so busy, she didn't even question that I was doing homework on a Friday night," Elise said.

"Mine either, but I often do homework on Friday nights, so it's not that big of a stretch."

Elise laughed.

"That's not funny," Coop protested.

"It is, but either way, I've got the key and the flour, so let's get going."

They went over their plan as they walked. They passed the sycamore tree that now had an empty scar where the face had been. Neither of them mentioned the change, and they fell silent as they approached the bakery.

Elise's heart raced as they peered into the small, dark windows, careful not to move too quickly to tip off anyone or anything that might be inside. A minute passed, but nothing moved.

"Are you sure you saw things floating around in here before?" Coop asked, his face still pressed to the glass.

"Are you sure you saw books flying off the shelves all by themselves at the library last night?" Elise asked in return.

"Good point," Coop said.

Elise was more annoyed they weren't seeing anything than with Coop's question. She had seen self-stirring bowls, last time, hadn't she? Or had she just—

"There!" she whispered to Coop as a light came on in the back room.

"I see it!" he whispered back.

A tray was floating out of the display case, and a broom was swishing about on its own, brushing the floors.

"Let's go!" Elise hissed. She took the key from her pocket and rattled the door open.

The broom whacked to the floor. The light in the kitchen went out.

"Pick up the broom and follow me," Elise told Coop.

He cautiously walked over to the broom and lifted it gingerly. Elise ran into the back room and turned on the kitchen lights. The room was silent and still.

Something had been here. Elise carefully took the bag of

flour from her pocket and spread its contents out on the floor. She and Coop then stood still, holding their breath, waiting. Come on, come on . . . The room remained still, the flour undisturbed. Elise thought for a moment before spreading her hands out wide. She slowly started walking through the part of the room without flour on the floor while waving her arms.

"Coop, do the same thing."

Coop nodded and began walking through the room, making wide circles with his arms. They covered the room slowly, edging closer and closer to the flour-covered half of the floor. Suddenly, a single small footprint appeared in the white powder.

"Oh!" Coop exclaimed.

A second footprint appeared in the flour, then a third and a fourth, and then many more.

"Now, Coop! Start swinging the broom in the air. Do it now!" Elise shouted

Coop stood frozen, holding the broom.

"Now, Coop!" Elise shouted again.

Coop snapped out of his shocked state and swung the broom. More footprints appeared in the flour, moving away from him. The footprints gathered in the corner, and Coop followed.

He swung the broom again and recoiled as he came into contact with something. Abruptly, a pointy, wide-brimmed hat fell to the ground, followed by a second pointed hat with no brim.

Before them stood what looked like a tiny man and woman in old-fashioned clothing. Their eyes were large in their small, round faces, and they blinked repeatedly. The man had on a button-down vest over a frilly white dress shirt and pants that stopped at his calves, bunching around his knees and thighs. The small woman wore a dress that reminded Elise of the early pilgrims and had her hair in a tight braid running down her back.

The man turned to the woman and began murmuring to her quickly with what sounded like a hint of anger. They ignored Elise and Coop as their discussion became more heated. Suddenly, the conversation stopped, and the woman pointed at them.

The small man grabbed a wooden spoon off of the counter, fury etched across his face. He began stomping toward Elise and Coop with the spoon raised in the air, and Elise stumbled back into Coop.

"Oh, nibbly bibbly, no!" a voice came from the back of the room as another light turned on. Wrapped in a quilted robe, Ms. Hopper trotted down the steps from the small apartment above the bakery. Lilah, the Corgi, tromped down behind her, barking.

"Jens! Put that spoon down right this minute!"

Lilah followed up with another sharp bark.

Ms. Hopper! Thank goodness! But the small man took another step forward. Elise pressed back further against Coop, who grunted, "Hey!" now squashed between her and the wall.

"Jens, do not be naughty. They are children who mean you no harm." Ms. Hopper spoke calmly now. The small female whispered to Jens as well, and whatever she said caught his attention.

The little man stopped stalking the children and stood with his arms crossed, tapping the spoon against his shoulder.

"Thank you, Freizen," Ms. Hopper said to the small

woman. She nodded toward Ms. Hopper but had not taken her eyes off Jens, still glaring murderously at Elise and Coop.

Ms. Hopper slowly crossed from the stairs to the stove and turned on a burner. She placed a pot on the open flame. Elise stared, mouth agape. Ms. Hopper took milk from the refrigerator and poured it into the pot along with what appeared to be powdered chocolate.

"Please, enjoy yourselves," Ms. Hopper said to the little couple, who eagerly grabbed spoons to stir the contents of the pot.

"And you children, good lordy jordy, follow me." Ms. Hopper turned and began walking back up the stairs with Lilah close behind. Elise and Coop edged away from the wall to follow. They kept as far as possible from the tiny man and woman who were now chattering excitedly as they spooned the hot chocolate into each other's mouth.

Ms. Hopper shook her head as they climbed the stairs. "I should have seen this coming after all your questions about goblins and kobolds."

ↄ

Ms. Hopper sat at her kitchen table, sipping from a cup of tea. "For the record, those were kobolds you just saw downstairs."

Elise and Coop sipped from their cups and nodded.

"I'll have to give them extra trinkets and treats to gain their trust again after this," Ms. Hopper said to herself under her breath. "Higgity biggity, what a mess."

"Sorry," Elise responded just above a whisper. It was real. It was all real. Coop remained silent, eyes still wide, sipping from his tea. "You were telling the truth about your helpers."

"Yes, I was."

"And I guess about the Cookbook too, then? How the spells and legends and gathered knowledge make the recipes better?"

"Yes, that as well," Ms. Hopper said. "If I just had it back . . . " She trailed off for a moment before continuing. "I could make my Goblin's Envy Pie or Black Forest Fairy Dumplings and . . . " She trailed off again.

"Well, then, we need to get it back before that critic comes in and does his review," Elise said. A positive review could save the bakery!

"Oh, googedly noogedly, we do need to get the Cookbook back, sweetie, but not for that reason. Having my recipes back would be great, but as I told you previously, the book contains a lot more than just recipes. Over the years it was used to gather and chronicle the natural and unnatural. There are witches' spells, enchantments, and the roots of legends contained within it. In the wrong hands, this information could be used for the wrong purposes." Ms. Hopper sighed. "In fact, oh heavenly bevenly, it appears it already has been."

"Wait," Coop interrupted. "Are we saying that trolls, goblins , and—and jogah stone throwers are real as well?"

"Yes, my dear. They're not hiding around every corner, but they are among us. They have been since the first people."

"I wonder if that's what we were attacked by at the library last night?" Coop asked, turning to Elise.

"Hold on—what do you mean the book is already being used for the wrong purposes?" Elise cut back in. "I thought you just misplaced it."

"Things haven't been right lately," Ms. Hopper said, her eyebrows drawing down into a V.

"What do you mean 'not right?'" Elise asked.

"Well, sometimes it's small things like plumbing backing up at higher rates than usual or Halloween decorations around town being turned upside down."

The vandalized decorations in the school gym, Elise thought.

"I saw that on Main street!" Coop said. "I was wondering why the witches were suddenly flying sideways and the mummies were unraveled."

"Goblins or jogah, as you called them," Ms. Hopper said. "They are emboldened, it seems, and have left some caution behind." She took another sip of her tea, and then the V formed again. "But more serious things are afoot. For example, although jogah are more neutral or good, that man accompanying Dr. Grout in the shop the other day was concerning."

"Yes?" Elise shivered at the thought of the large, strange man.

"Well, that was no man—that was a troll. I couldn't see his tail—he had hidden it well—but he couldn't hide that smell."

"A troll?" Coop put down his teacup, nearly spilling it.

"I didn't smell anything—maybe a little musty, I guess, like a teenage boy," Elise said, making sure not to look in Coop's direction.

"I've smelled enough of them to know. You learn to recognize it." Ms. Hopper nodded her head and the hair tower tilted back and forth.

"Wasn't it a little small for a troll?" Coop asked. "From the things that I've read, I thought they were, you know, bigger or hiding under bridges and stuff."

"You can find some under dark bridges, but they can be found in all sorts of places," Ms. Hopper responded. "As to size, they come in all sorts of sizes as well, and they all have unnatural strength. Some are the size of large humans and disguise themselves so they can move about among us. Others can be huge." Ms. Hopper raised her hands high above her for emphasis before continuing.

"They can be fifty feet tall or even the height of small mountains. Those rarely move, and if they do, it's in the middle of the night. Some only wake up every hundred years or so and then roam the earth for a short while and feed before going back to sleep and turning back to rock until they wake once more."

"Wait," Coop said. "According to our research last night, trolls, or stone coats, can't come out in the sunlight. You said you saw it the other day. How can that be?"

"That's part of what convinced us that Dr. Grout had the Cookbook," Ms. Hopper said. "That book is one of the only places that has spells of protection that would allow a troll to move about during the day without fear of the sun's rays turning it to stone."

"Uh huh," Coop muttered, deep in thought.

"Who's 'us'?" Elise asked.

"Oh, nibbly bibbly." Ms. Hopper thought for a moment before answering. "I guess you know enough at this point to tell you more."

"Tell us what?" Elise pressed.

Ms. Hopper looked at her for a moment longer before answering.

"About the October Society."

"The what?" Elise said. Was this some sort of secret society?

"It's a gathering of people who have common . . . interests."

"Like what?" Coop asked.

"Well, they are especially sensitive to the natural . . . and the unnatural. They have taken the time to educate themselves beyond the boundaries of everyday life and to bond with the natural world around them." Ms. Hopper paused, her gaze growing distant.

"What does that mean?" Coop asked. His fingers twitched, and Elise had to grin. He looked like he wanted to take notes.

"These people, they don't just see nature. They study how it weaves and connects the world around us. They see the details that most people miss, or at least they try to."

"They're—magic?" Elise asked. Her heart thumped.

"No, not really magic. That's just a word people use for something they can't understand or explain. These people are more interested in living in harmony with nature and the spiritual world. They have a natural affinity for it but they also try to learn from it and use the remedies and knowledge it provides to live in balance. For some, the goal is to protect the vulnerable from those that would do harm or take advantage of nature for their own selfish interests." Ms. Hopper nodded to herself.

"Native Americans have their own stories about shamans and wizards," Coop said. "They passed them down generation to generation. Like the ones about the jogah I mentioned."

"Yes," Ms. Hopper said. "I know them well. Little elf-like creatures who emerge from the ground, or the stone coats who tread across the earth like thunder, much like the trolls of European legend."

"What you're saying is the same as we read last night. It just seems like a lot of this stuff and these creatures are rooted in the old stories," Elise said.

"You're correct. Some came across the ocean with the first European settlers and African slaves or some were already here, according to Native American oral stories."

"OK," Elise said. "I get what you're saying, but—" and here her heart fluttered up into her throat "—you've claimed to be a witch a time or two. Is that true as well?"

"Shipity witchity, yes."

"So, you, like, fly around on a broom and eat children?" Elise asked, her voice rising to a near squeak. Ms. Hopper couldn't possibly do that!

"Oh, don't be so dramatic," Ms. Hopper said a little sharply. "And that is a little insulting. A witch is a person who practices their beliefs, some dark, some light, but most simply in tune with nature, using rituals, incantations, abilities, and knowledge they have gained over the years. Every peoples has its version."

Elise swallowed. "What kind of witch are you?"

"Hmm." Ms. Hopper tilted her head. "I'm more about being in harmony with nature and protecting others. I also love to use the gifts of the earth to bake my special goods and bring joy to the people who come to my shop. I wasn't always a great baker, but when the Cookbook was passed down to me, I studied it and the arts until I could perform enchantments and spells to benefit those around me."

"What other kind of witches are there?" Coop asked.

"Oh, there are those tied to nature—white magic and dark magic, as non-practitioners call it, and even necromancers who try to raise the dead. I know some spirit-binding spells and such but none of that raise-the-dead stuff. I wouldn't think of it."

"What other types of people, besides witches, are in this October Society?" Elise asked.

"Well, there are the witches' covens as you mentioned." Ms. Hopper put her hand up in the air and started counting her fingers.

"Are all of the witches in covens women?" Elise asked.

"Around here they are, but if you go to the big cities and other countries, there are male ones called warlocks or high doctors sometimes."

"Oh." Elise's mind spun with all this new information.

Ms. Hopper went back to counting on her fingers. "And then there are Indian shamans or wizards, as Coop said." She moved to the next finger. "Then there are voodoo doctors and various holy men, and that's about it." She thought for another moment with still one finger uncounted. "Oh, and the blacksmiths—we mostly call them plumbers nowadays." She nodded her head again in satisfaction.

"Plumbers? Like the guys who fix pipes and leaks?" Coop was incredulous.

"Yes, plumbers." Ms. Hopper smiled. "They're in touch with the innards of most towns and cities like the blacksmiths of old. They're the traffic cops and the librarians for what's happening in the unseen parts of the city. They literally work at the crossroads of major pipe junctures and tunnels. They know what lies below."

"I—I'm not sure what to think about that," Coop stammered.

"In fact," Ms. Hopper continued, "I'm meeting with the Plumber tomorrow—" She cut herself off and looked away.

"Tomorrow?" Elise prompted.

"Nothing—forget about it."

"Please tell us," Elise said.

"Jeepers creepers, I think I am getting senile. Can hardly keep anything to myself anymore." Two pink spots appeared on Ms. Hopper's cheekbones.

"Ms. Hopper, I need to go with you," Elise insisted.

"But you're not ready."

"You said yourself that some people learn to see the unseen through gaining knowledge. Well, this is the kind of knowledge I need, especially now." Elise pleaded.

"But . . . " Ms. Hopper sputtered.

"And I'm in too!" Coop said. "I can explain to Elise the things she doesn't understand during the meeting."

"Coop!" Elise glared at him.

"Just kidding, just kidding." Coop bent over the table, laughing.

"You better be." Elise couldn't contain a smile.

"Oh, noogly googly," Ms. Hopper said under her breath. "I guess it isn't too early for you to begin your second education, so to speak."

"Yes!" both exclaimed.

"But you are just there to listen. You stay quiet and take in knowledge. You do not discuss what you hear or see with anyone." Ms. Hopper was quiet for a second, letting her words sink in.

"Come by the bakery after school tomorrow, and we'll walk over to the meeting. I'll let them know ahead of time that I'm bringing you." Miss Hopper, stared at them sternly. "Don't make me regret this because then I'll have to do that whole eating children thing you mentioned."

Elise nodded, not entirely sure whether or not Ms. Hopper was joking about that last part.

TAYLOR PENSONEAU

CHAPTER EIGHT

Eggs and Bacon

From the journal of Niles Folsom, High Doctor, October Society of
New York City

Thursday, October 29, 1986, Legend Hollow, New York

*E*ver more urgent reports continue to come in from the field.
*Pumpkin headed scarecrow sentries have been unusually
active carrying out their duties. Goblin music can be heard
carried on the winds, and terrifying shrieks are emanating from
the outlying woods. Many people have stated that their dogs are
on edge and their cats refuse to chase their tails. A captured troll
was returned to stone, but before it took its last breath, it confessed
to Society members that the Cookbook is indeed now being stored
underground beneath Legend Hollow, protected by multiple
November Men and their followers. As the all-important All
Hallows Eve Jamboree is just around the corner, the Cookbook*

must be recovered right away. A plan shall be discussed this afternoon at a meeting of the Legend Hollow chapter of the Society taking place at the Plumber's place of business.

Elise awoke early and made breakfast for the family. She wanted to give her mother a break since she had a morning shift.

"Well, doesn't this look nice? Coffee and everything." Elise's mother smiled as she poured herself a cup.

"Stephen, breakfast is ready!" she called, taking a seat next to Elise with a plateful of eggs and bacon. Stephen slid into a seat next to her.

"I miss this. This is nice." Elise's mother looked around the table.

"Miss what?" Stephen asked, snatching the remaining pieces of bacon.

"Oh, you know, just this . . . " Elise's mother drifted off without finishing her sentence.

Elise knew what she meant and missed it too.

"It's OK, mom. You can say you miss us eating together like this." She paused. "Like with Dad. Like having the whole family together when you didn't have to work so many shifts."

Elise's mother did not answer but instead put her fork down and slid her hand over Elise's. "By the way, I need you to take Stephen to the bakery after school since I won't be home until dinnertime. He can stay there and do his homework while you work."

"But Mom, I've got something after school before work." She couldn't miss the October Society meeting!

"Well, Stephen will have to go with you."

"But—"

"No buts, Elise. We all have to pitch in."

"I'm not a baby," Stephen said. "You let me go to D&D night by myself."

"Coop is with you on those nights."

"But—" Stephen tried again.

"No buts from you either, and did you do your music homework last night—your note memorization? I didn't see you practice."

"Yes. I read over it once. I've got it."

Stephen was so lucky. "I wish I had that ability," Elise said.

"What?" Stephen said, although he knew the answer. He just liked to hear others acknowledge it.

"Your gift for memorization. So unfair that you can just look at something once and have it memorized."

"It is nice, isn't it?" Stephen grinned and stuffed another slice of bacon into his mouth.

જી

On the walk to school, both Elise and Stephen were silent for the first couple of blocks until they passed the sycamore trees. Elise avoided the ghastly scar and instead kept her eyes forward.

"Why are you acting weird?" Stephen asked.

"What do you mean?" Elise mumbled.

"I mean, you usually don't care if I tag along to the bakery or whatever."

"Don't take it personally. It's just that . . . " Elise trailed off.

"What?"

"Well, you know how strange things have been happening

lately? Like how I told you about that weird man at the bakery?"

"I guess."

"And like what happened at the library the other night?"

"That was wild," Stephen said. He began to drag his violin case.

"And all of the crazy stuff that has been happening around town?" Elise continued.

"You mean all the Halloween pranks the kids have been pulling?"

"I think it's more than that. I think all of these things might be connected, and there's a group of people Ms. Hopper knows that think so too. She calls them the October Society."

"Huh?"

"This Society is meeting today after school, and Coop and I were invited to the meeting. I guess since you're with me this afternoon, you'll have to go with us."

"Cool," Stephen said, smiling.

"And quit dragging your violin case."

❧

After school, Elise and Coop waited for Stephen outside the music room. It was next to the boiler room in the basement, and Elise wondered if the frequent clunks and clangs of the boilers or Sam's colorful language ever affected the musicians in the next room.

The boiler room door opened, and maintenance man Sam himself emerged, mumbling under his breath. When he spotted Elise and Coop, he caught himself and stopped.

"Sorry, kids—the old girls are giving me a real battle

today." He poked a thumb over his shoulder toward the boilers.

Elise and Coop craned their heads toward the opening of the forbidden room, hoping to get a quick look inside. Sam blocked most of their view by standing in the doorway, but Elise could still see around part of him. Oddly enough, another man crawled from a hatch in the ground. Had the school hired an extra maintenance man? She wondered if Coop saw him too.

The other man had on a red coat and a black hat. He reminded her of an old British soldier or something. Before Elise could get another look, Sam closed the door behind him.

"They just get lazier the older they get. I give 'em a little whack now and then to remind 'em who's boss." Sam's mustache curved to match his smile, exposing startlingly white teeth. "You kids have a good afternoon," he said, heading off down the hallway.

Stephen appeared from the music room, and the three left for the bakery.

"Well, whatly duttly!" Ms. Hopper exclaimed upon their arrival when she saw Stephen accompanying Elise and Coop.

"It couldn't be helped," Elise apologized. "My mom said I had to watch him this afternoon."

"I guess you expect him to go with us to the meeting, then?" Ms. Hopper's towering coiffeur tilted to the side. She ran her hands over her long gown. "At this point, it won't be much of a secret society if we just bring the whole town along."

"He's the last one, Ms. Hopper. I promise," Elise said.

"Well, I guess he would have found out eventually. This is the last one, though," Ms. Hopper said sternly.

TAYLOR PENSONEAU

CHAPTER NINE

The October Society

The Plumber's shop was located on Main Street only two blocks from the bakery. It sat behind the dreaded sycamore trees who were doing their usual swaying and giving off their faintly sweet scent. They obscured most of the storefront, but the building's odd angles, roof line, and multiple chimneys still poked up behind them. It was like a jigsaw puzzle that didn't quite fit right together as if its creator had been struck each day with a new idea during its construction and had followed that whim wherever it took him.

Elise stood for a moment, not sure if she wanted to enter the shop now that she was there. She looked over her shoulder at the trees, including the one with the scar. It was so . . . weird. She couldn't look at the scar for long and instead averted her eyes to the base of the tree.

She blinked several times, focusing on something odd. Was it . . . a tiny door? It was only inches tall, nestled in the base of the tree. Its outline barely stood out from the rest of the tree trunk.

"Let's go. What are we waiting for?" Stephen whined, snapping Elise back to attention. She followed the group up to the front door, surprised at her own reluctance.

A small sign on one of the front windows stated plumbing services with a phone number stenciled below it. Elise had never noticed before, but the windows were blacked out. Her stomach tightened.

They were the first to arrive. Inside, it was so hot that she instantly started sweating. Large pipes of different sizes and colors ran along the ceiling, walls, and floor in every direction. Some were emitting small plumes of steam, and others made clanking sounds. There were also small manhole covers and hatches embedded into the floor here and there. Most had padlocks or bars across them. To keep people from opening them? Elise wondered. Or to keep something below out?

The room looked like some sort of crazy crossroads or intersection. It seemed every pipe in the city was passing through this room. Coop looked impressed, and Stephen whistled under his breath.

A short man with long, hairy arms, dark skin, and an overly muscular chest emerged from the back room. He clenched a brown pipe in the corner of his mouth, and a full beard hid his neck. An unkempt afro shot from the top of his head in all directions.

"Enough of that!" he yelled, banging a wrench on one of the large, clanking pipes. "Back underground you go." The sounds from the pipe ceased although dozens of other loud pops and hisses continued echoing around the large room.

The man's gaze moved to the visitors. "So, these are the children you told me about, huh?"

"They are," Ms. Hopper said with a slight bow. "Children, this is Franklin Johnson. We call him the Plumber."

"Because I am." A smile split the Plumber's beard.

A plume of steam or smoke—Elise wasn't sure which—began shooting from beneath a loose screw in a rusted pipe that ran along the far wall. The Plumber ignored the hissing sound and instead offered the group a seat at a round table in the center of the room.

As Elise sat, she was startled to see two small men, similar to the kobolds at Ms. Hopper's bakery, enter the room. One was slightly taller than the other and wore wooden shoes while the shorter man wore knee-high boots. They both had long noses and beards, similar to the kobolds at Ms. Hopper's bakery, and were clothed in the same eighteenth-century style. They scurried over to the hissing pipe and began turning the large screws with tools they carried in their small hands.

"Jeepers!" Stephen shouted.

The Plumber looked at him in surprise.

"Oh, shibbity nibbity," Ms. Hopper said. "I forgot that young Stephen has never seen a kobold before. I had told Mr. Johnson that it was OK for them to come out and show themselves during the meeting." She tapped the side of her head. "Further proof that the old melon ain't what it used to be."

"This was part of the strange stuff I was telling you about, Stephen." Elise put her hand on his shoulder. "It's all right. They're friendly as long as you treat them nicely."

The kobold with the wooden shoes glanced at Stephen and nodded slightly before turning back to working on the screw. He twisted until the hissing steam stopped emerging from the pipe. The two small men then holstered their tools and headed back out of the room with the taller kobold's wooden shoes clacking against the concrete floor until they were gone.

"OK, that was unexpected," Stephen said, his eyes wide.

The front door opened and Bill Black from Black's Hardware entered, wearing his rumpled purple wizard hat. The hat suddenly didn't seem so strange anymore, Elise realized, compared to everything else she'd seen lately.

"Bill!" Coop said with a smile, waving.

Stephen, who had managed to recover, waved as well.

"Hello, fellow gamers." Bill took a seat at the table.

"I didn't know you were part of a group like this," Coop said.

"Well, now you do." Bill crossed his arms and said nothing further.

"OK, then." Stephen said.

"Look, I wasn't in favor of bringing kids into the group, if you must know. Especially now during this time of heightened danger."

"Fresh blood is needed, Bill, you know that," Ms. Hopper responded. "I'm not getting any younger, and the next generation must be brought in even if it is a little earlier than we intended."

"Yeah, yeah," Bill said. "Well, if you're going to join the October Society, you should know that many of our D&D campaigns were for the purpose of simulating different battle plans. I was testing out scenarios for the Society. If it worked on paper, there was a better chance it would work in real life when we took on a troll or bad witch or what have you, I figured."

"Really?" Stephen mused out loud. "Hmm. Like when we fought the goblins in the Black Forest?"

"Yes." Bill uncrossed his arms and leaned forward. "We had that gang of goblins on the run with our show of force and the trickery we employed. In fact, it played out nearly the same when we recently took some o near the edge of town." A smile spread across his face.

"Wait—what?" Coop asked.

The front door opened again, and a grey-haired woman entered.

"Ms. Thorstad!" Elise whispered excitedly.

"Hello, Ellen. Thank you for joining us today." Ms. Hopper smiled at her old friend.

"Of course. I wanted to meet our new recruits." She winked at Elise and sat down next to her.

"Is Ms. Thorstad a witch?" Stephen whispered to Elise.

"Yes," Ms. Thorstad whispered before Elise could answer.

"A good kind of witch?" He asked.

"Of course!" Ms. Hopper answered from across the table. Ms. Thorstad smiled.

The door opened once more, and in came George First carrying a terrifying mask painted in vibrant reds, browns, and whites. Stephen nearly jumped out of his seat. Elise's heart leaped to her throat before she realized it was made from the carving in the sycamore tree.

"George, your false face mask is scaring the children," Ms. Thorstad scolded.

"Sorry," he said quietly.

"It's OK, Mr. First. I—I knew it was just a false face,"

Coop stammered.

George took a seat at the table, placing his mask face down next to him. Stephen settled back into his chair but kept an eye on the mask.

"Ahem, looks like we're all here. Let's go ahead and get started," Mr. Johnson said. He did not sit with the others but instead kept banging on various pipes and making adjustments here and there.

A gatekeeper, Elise thought. Maybe even a conductor of sorts.

Suddenly, a flap in a large pipe opened, and a small green hand with long, cruel-looking claws took a swipe at the Plumber before he slammed the flap shut.

"As you all know, a troll was captured last week in broad daylight," the Plumber said, leaning against the pipe flap. "He was as dumb as the proverbial rock we turned him into. But the fact that he was out in daylight was very concerning."

"I was there," George First said. "I used my mask to trick him, making him believe I was another troll. I got him to give me the details of the enchantment protecting him from the sunlight. Ms. Thorstad was then able to reverse the spell." George looked at Ms. Thorstad, who nodded.

One of the manholes in the floor began straining against the metal bar locking it down. Green hands and claws squirmed through the small gap beneath the lid. Mr. Johnson calmly walked across the room and stood upon the manhole until the claws retreated and the lid clamped back down.

"Now," he continued as if nothing had occurred, "a spirit was recently summoned and set loose upon the town. A member of the Society captured it earlier today. Apparently, the spirit was a British soldier from the war of 1812. But, you know what? Let him tell you himself."

The Plumber picked up a book from a nearby desk, then slapped it onto the table.

"A History of the War of 1812?" Coop asked.

"Yes, we used it to bind the spirit." The Plumber thumbed through the book until he found a painting of British soldiers and nodded to Ms. Hopper.

"Hidey ho, you are released from below, Mr. Gerald," Ms. Hopper chanted, waving her hand above the book. "Please come forth from the page."

Elise's heart pounded, and she looked around the table at the calm faces of the Society members, wishing she felt the same. Suddenly, streaks of color, first reds, then black and white, began rising from the picture. The colors swirled until a figure formed next to the table.

The uniform was indeed that of a soldier from the early 1800s. It was dirty in spots and bore dried blood on the right side of the chest. The dull red stood out from the bright red of his long jacket. Elise tried not to stare at the stain and looked away quickly when she noticed that the soldier was looking directly back at her.

"Mr. Gerald, welcome back. We've gathered the Society to hear your story," the Plumber said, folding his hairy arms.

"Sir." Mr. Gerald saluted stiffly.

"No need for that," Bill Black said.

"Yes, Sir. Er, I mean, yes." Mr. Gerald nearly saluted again before catching himself. "Well, what I means to say is that I was enjoying my rest in Polstein Cemetery—you know, with the war being over for me and all—and then the next thing I knows is that I was pulled from me grave and summed to a large cave or underground room with lots of shiny things and little green creatures running about."

"The Goblin Market," Ms. Hopper said.

"That's what we thought as well. Not many places have so many of the little green creatures gathered all at once," the Plumber agreed.

"Goblins?" Stephen's voice squeaked. "Like the little green claws trying to make their way out of that pipe flap over there a moment ago?"

"Yes," Ms. Thorstad answered. "Goblins are nature at its worst."

"They were once kobolds," Ms. Hopper explained. "Often they are turned into malevolent creatures by the cruelty or tricks of humans, and sometimes they are just kobolds with damaged souls who evolve into corrupt things over time."

"There were many of those indeed in this place. But there were regular humans there as well." Mr. Gerald looked down at the stain on his chest, attempting to wipe it away.

"Can you describe these humans?" Ms. Thorstad asked.

"There were three as far as I could tell. I couldn't really make out the first person. Never made a peep, and all I could see was arms aholding a book. The rest of him or her was in shadow behind a rock column. Then there was a great plump fellow. A stomach so big, I don't know how he kept upright. He had a big man with him with a large nose and funny outfit."

"That's surely Dr. Grout and probably his troll, James." Ms. Hopper's hair tower trembled as she shook her head.

"Well, ma'am, I'm not sure, but I do know that the fat man shouted a lot of commands at me that I didn't understand, and he grew quite exasperated," Mr. Gerald said. "The one time the other one spoke, it whispered something to the plump fellow about me not being a wicked enough spirit and they had not done the spell right from the book or some such."

"That can happen if you don't have the right skill level." Ms. Hopper smiled with pride at Ms. Thorstad.

"Sounds to me like they knackered it up," Ms. Thorstad said.

"I don't know about all that, but I'm no bad spirit, I can tell you that much," Mr. Gerald said. "Did my duty for the King and all but not bad, plus I'm not going to be ordered around by no colonists. Anyway, after a while, the plump fellow yells some more and says they should release me and try again. Then they just up and leave the big room and the book sitting on a table and me standing there. I wasn't sure what to do with myself among the swarm of little green creatures and their piles of silverware and coins and whatnot, so I wandered off, I did." Mr. Gerald nodded and brushed at his stain once again before continuing.

"There was an opening in the rock wall leading from the room, so I wandered out. Soon enough, it led to a tunnel. I roamed the tunnels for a day until I emerged in some large building with lots of kids running about. Maybe a big school, I think."

"Hay Edwards! I knew I saw you!" Coop exclaimed. He smacked Elise on the shoulder.

"I wandered through this Hay Edwards, as you call it, until I found my way out and started looking for the old Tilted Lantern Tavern. I remembered having a good evening there with a pint and a nice fire before my final battle.

"I found the tavern by instinct, like a homing pigeon, I did. Only there was a different building where it should have been, and it had a different name, but it did look like a right proper tavern, so I bellied up to the bar and waited for the serving wench."

"It was Boon's Saloon over on Third Street. Scared the patrons half to death, I might add," Ms. Thorstad said. "The Society got wind of the spirit, and the Plumber and I went there after hours and bound him to the history book, and here we are."

"Mr. Gerald, do you think you could identify that book and room again if we got you back to the Goblin Market?" George First asked.

"Probably. Perhaps you could release me back to Polstein Cemetery to be with my mates afterwards in exchange."

A sharp whistling sound came from a pipe along the floor, catching Elise's ear. As she watched, a trickle of clear liquid began to leak from the elbow joint. A human-like creature only a few inches tall emerged from what looked all too much like a mouse hole where the wall met the floor.

"Oh, would you look at that—an elf," Mr. Gerald said smiling. "We've got two of them living in trees over at the cemetery."

The tiny door she had seen in the sycamore tree outside!

"That doesn't look like an elf. At least not the D&D kind," Stephen whispered to Coop.

"A jogah," Coop said back.

George First nodded in agreement. "In Iroquois oral traditions, they guard against poisonous snakes and creatures that try to escape from the underworld."

"In Western culture, some people call them fairies while others call them elves, sometimes gnomes even," Bill said as the creature hurried silently to the whistling pipe. It slapped some sort of patch on the pipe, and the leaking ceased.

"They live in trees, gardens, underground, or the woods, but some, like this little fellow, have taken a shine to living in human structures," Mr. Johnson said.

The elf wiped its small hands upon an apron and returned to its hole.

"Back to the matter at hand." The Plumber rolled a large map out onto the table. Elise craned her neck to see it. legend hollow underground was written in block letters at the top. It resembled a blueprint on thick white paper with what appeared to be dozens of drainage tunnels, passageways, sewers, mine shafts, and irregular rooms.

Wow. She had heard about the abandoned coal mine tunnels running beneath the city and Washington Park, but so many? They seemed to crisscross everywhere.

"The most direct route to the Goblin Market is from Hell's Gate in Washington Park, but it's guarded by a large troll and a pack of goblins," the Plumber continued.

"This particular pack of goblins is said to be the direct descendants of the goblins that led Rip Van Winkle astray," Ms. Thorstad added.

"The entrance below Hay Edwards School is the next most direct route to the underground and the Goblin Market. It's in the school boiler room," the Plumber said, pointing to the marked entrance on the map. "We head to the Market, get the book back from Dr. Grout, and get back out through the tunnels as quickly as possible. In fact, since Hell's Gate is only guarded from the outside, we could use the element of surprise and use it to exit from the underground. They aren't expecting anyone to be coming out of Hell's Gate."

"Waity fraity—who exactly is on the roster for this little adventure? I assume you and George First and Bill Black?"

Ms. Hopper said, glancing at Elise and the other kids. Mr. Gerald followed her glance.

"That's the way I game-planned it, Ms. Hopper," Bill said. "But if we enter the tunnels on a school day, it'll look a little strange for three unknown men to be wandering the halls, so we thought the kids could guide us to the boiler room. If someone questions us, we could claim we're their parents or something."

"I can't go, but that's the plan," the Plumber said. "I've got my hands full here at the crossroads." He pointed at the shaking pipes and banging metal flaps all around the room. "As it is, I've given up sleeping just to keep the creepy crawlies at bay."

"I wish I could go, but I'm in charge of the jamboree for All Hollows Eve," Ms. Thorstad said. "I'll be leading the efforts to monitor the barrier between the living and the dead all night."

"Yes, yes, I understand. I would go, but these days I think I would be more hindrance than help crawling about underground on my hands and knees," Ms. Hopper said sadly.

The image of Ms. Hopper's pillar of hair scraping along the tunnel roofs popped into Elise's mind.

"It looks like it'll be just George and Bill, then, with the kids guiding them to the entrance below the school," the Plumber said. "They will also have Mr. Gerard help them find the book. And I propose sending an elf with them to assist once they're in the tunnels."

As if he had been listening, the tiny elf emerged once again from his mouse hole. He turned toward the group, took off his pointy green hat, and bowed so low that his beard nearly scraped the ground.

"Nigrim here," he squeaked in a voice barely audible above the clamor of the clanging pipes.

"Wouldn't you feel safer with maybe a kobold or two?" Coop asked, looking doubtfully at the tiny elf.

"Can't," George First said.

The elf glared at Coop and crossed his small arms.

"Why not?" Coop pressed.

"Because trolls and goblins can smell kobolds and dwarfs from two hundred yards away. The mission would be over the moment they entered the tunnels," Bill said. "Elves have learned to mask their scent, though. Trolls can hardly see or hear them, and they certainly can't smell them."

"Sure," Nigrim said in his high-pitched voice. "Little lavender rub here, little rosemary or sage rub there, and elf scent, it disappear." Nigrim waived his little arms in the air for emphasis.

Elise had to swallow a giggle. Coop threw her a glance, eyebrows raised, and she cleared her throat and sat up straighter, giggles gone.

"And he can guide you?" Elise asked Bill and George.

"Can. With this." Nigrim reached into his pocket and pulled out a miniature lantern glowing with a tiny flame that cast light throughout the room.

"It's a firework ember he caught and kept from last summer's 4th of July celebration downtown," Bill said.

"Huh." Stephen said looking at the ember.

"This is all well and good, but I still do not agree that the children should be involved," Ms. Hopper cut in.

"I agree," Ms. Thorstad added.

"Look, all they're doing is getting us to the underground

entrance at the school. If there are any summoned spirits, trolls, or anything else guarding the entrance, then we'll send the children away and deal with them on our own," Bill responded.

"Wait a minute," Coop said. "This sounds a lot like our D&D campaign last week where we had to gain entrance to the underground Caverns of Calamity by getting past the Minotaur."

"It should," Bill said, tipping his wizard's hat sideways, a smug smile on his face.

"I might point out that my magic user, Orlem, nearly died getting past that minotaur," Coop said. "I think he only had two hit points left at the end." Coop's voice trailed off.

"Still worked."

Coop opened his mouth as if to protest, but Stephen cut in. "We have a half day tomorrow, on account of Saturday being Halloween and Friday being the last day of school before the holiday. The day is pretty much going to be a blow-off with the students getting to wear costumes and the classroom parties and all."

"He's right. We can meet you at the front steps at noon and take you into the school from there," Elise said.

"Fine, the children can take you as far as the entrance to the underground, and then they are to go straight home after that," Ms. Hopper insisted.

"Of course," Bill said.

Nigrim nodded his small head as well, then tucked away his lamp with the fireworks ember and headed back through his tiny door.

"In fact, the less they know about the rest of this escapade, the better," Ms. Hopper added, nodding toward the map.

"Right," the Plumber replied. Elise was still straining to read the map, but he rolled it up before she could look at it further.

"Okey dokey, it's time for you to head home. Have some dinner and get a good night's rest." Ms. Hopper stood up.

"Agreed." Bill Black readjusted his wizard's hat. "Coop, George and I will meet you guys tomorrow at the front steps of the school at noon."

"Yes, sir!" Stephen said, standing up and saluting. Bill ignored him.

"And you Mr. Gerald, you can jump back into the book until summoned again." Ms. Hopper indicated with a nod towards the open book.

"Madame," Mr. Gerald responded, snapping off a salute matching Stephen's.

Elise slung her backpack over her shoulders. "Are you sure we can't help more? I'm sure we could help in the tunnels."

"Yeah, and I've already kind of trained for it by playing the D&D campaigns with Bill," Stephen added.

"Sorry, children, but no." Ms. Hopper was firm. Her hair swayed forward emphatically.

✧

They walked in silence for a block before Elise spoke.

"I don't like being treated this. We're just trying to help, and they're treating us like grade schoolers. No offense, Stephen."

"None taken," Stephen respoded.

"I could have memorized the route if I could have seen that map for a little longer," Coop said.

"I can help with that," Stephen offered.

"What do you mean?" Coop asked.

"The map. Stop for a second, and give me a notepad and something to write with."

Coop pulled a notebook and pencil from his backpack, and Stephen sat down on the sidewalk. Elise looked over his shoulder and gaped as he began forming lines into tunnels, passageways, and drains.

"Wow!" Coop whispered.

"I know," Elise said as she watched the town's entire underground emerge before them.

CHAPTER TEN

A Witch, a Ghost, and a Clown

From the journal of Niles Folsom, High Doctor, October Society of
New York City

Friday, October 30, 1986, Legend Hollow, New York

*I*t is the day before All Hallows Eve, and increased mischief
is afoot. The barrier between the living world and the other
continues to thin. The grave of the Hessian has been disturbed,
and crows scream from the treetops. Thankfully, members of the
Society have confirmed that the bones of the Hessian, including
his detached head and his horse companion, are complete and
still in the earth. We don't know what was intended, but this
appears to be the failed work of the November Men. It is assumed
that they have moved on to other nefarious goals. The urgency to
recover the Cookbook rises . . .

A witch, a ghost, and a clown which dragged a violin case walked the final block to school without speaking or noting the costumes of the other children around them. The morning classes were a blur, and before Elise knew it, the bell signaling the end of the half day rang out.

She pushed past a boy dressed as President Ronald Reagan and another dressed as the wrestler Hulk Hogan. A girl named Emily in an Elvira costume complimented Elise's witch costume, and Elise returned the sentiment before rushing to the front steps.

Coop and Stephen were already there, waiting with Bill Black and George First. Coop had removed his white ghost sheet, having stuffed it in his backpack, but Stephen still wore his full clown costume except for the shoes. Elise yanked off her high-heeled boots and switched them out for tennis shoes. She stuffed the boots and her tall, pointy hat into her backpack.

Bill had removed his hat and George kept his mask tucked under his right arm. Funny—with everyone else dressed in costume, they would have fit right in for once.

"Hello, Mr. Black, Mr. First," Elise said. "All set?" A couple of inches of the rolled-up map poked out the top flap of Bill's military-grade backpack, and two small eyes peered out of the opening. Nigrim. She gave him a wink and thought she saw him wink back.

"Yes. If you could lead, we'll be underway," Bill said.

Luckily, a girls' basketball game was taking place after school, so Bill and George somewhat fit in with the other parents walking toward the gymnasium. Elise, Coop, and Stephen led the men down the marble steps to the basement.

Elise breathed easier when they entered the hallway where the boiler room was located and saw it was empty of students and teachers.

"This is it," Stephen said, pointing to a grey metal door. "Hopefully, it's not locked."

Bill opened his backpack and fished out his wizard's hat, putting it back atop his head in its rightful spot. He looked more like the Bill Elise knew. "Let me give it a try."

He turned the handle, and the door creaked open. But before he could push it all the way, it swung open on its own. Standing in the opening was maintenance man Sam.

He yelled something Elise couldn't understand, but he sure looked angry. He was breathing heavily, and his eyes looked glazed over. Something was wrong.

Sam took an unsteady step toward Bill and raised his hands as if to grab Bill's neck. Bill jerked back.

"Bill, look at this forehead," George shouted. A black X marked the center of Sam's brow. It looked like it was made of ash or some other similar material.

"A hex! he's been possessed!" George slipped on his false face mask and lunged between the kids and Sam. Elise stumbled back. A hex? Who did this? Sam took no notice of the mask and instead kept advancing slowly toward Bill, who retreated across the hallway until his back was against the wall.

"Finish him!" yelled a voice from down the hallway. Dr. Grout waddled around the corner followed by his troll, James. He was holding something—a small doll in his right hand and a book in his left.

"Keep them from your boiler room!" Dr. Grout shouted at the doll in his hand. "They don't belong here!"

Dr. Grout had finally dispensed with hiding his intentions. Elise tried to push Stephen behind her, but he squirmed away. Sam gave another angry shout, grabbing Bill's shoulder.

"James!" Dr. Grout turned to his troll. "Smash the Indian and the children."

The troll began lumbering toward the group with his horrible, gangly strides, the ski pants making their awful swishing sound.

Elise smothered a scream as George ran toward the oncoming troll, growling behind his mask. James stopped in his tracks. A look of confusion spread across his face.

"You stupid beast!" Dr. Grout screamed. "It's just a mask!"

The troll blinked its heavily lidded eyes as Sam leaped at Bill and grabbed his neck.

"No!" Elise cried.

A familiar sound approached from down the hall. The clinking and clanking of many keys came into focus, and a large figure with a bushy mustache rushed towards them Mr. Hernandez!

"You leave them alone!" Mr. Hernandez shouted. He swung his fist at Dr. Grout, landing a blow to his shoulder.

Dr. Grout cried out in shock and pain, the doll dropping from his right hand and bouncing on the floor. Immediately, Sam removed his hands from Bill's throat. He stared at his still trembling hands wide eyed, clearly confused.

Bill put his own hands to his throat, gasping deep breaths. Sam shook his head as if trying to wake himself up. He appeared to be in a fog as he wandered away down the hall and up the stairs, heading out of Elise's view.

The troll roared with rage seeing Dr. Grout struck by Mr. Hernandez. He wheeled about, forgetting George First and his mask. He stomped toward Mr. Hernandez, swinging a massive fist. Mr. Hernandez managed to raise his arm to block the blow, but the resulting crack made Elise feel sick to her stomach. Mr. Hernandez groaned and collapsed, his forearm bent at an unnatural angle.

"Mr. Hernandez!" Coop dashed to the handyman's side.

Bill ran toward the boiler room door. Dr. Grout pointed at Bill and yelled for James to stop him. Mr. Hernandez was clearly no longer a threat, so the troll turned away. With his long, lurching steps, the troll caught up to Bill and yanked him away from the door. Dr. Grout rushed over to them. He still carried the book in his left hand—The Legend of Sleepy Hollow, Elise noted.

She grabbed Stephen's hand and hurried to Mr. Hernandez.

"My arm is broken. We need to get out of here." He hissed, wincing with pain as the kids helped him to his feet.

Elise glanced over at Bill, who was backing away from the boiler room door and its troll guard. Nigrim's head poked out of Bill's pack as the elf said something to him in a series of squeaks.

"Elf!" the troll roared.

"Yes, elf," Dr. Grout confirmed from the boiler room entryway. "You need to smash the wizard, the Indian, and the children, and then you can eat the elf."

What? Dr. Grout was offering up Nigrim as a troll treat?

James grunted approvingly, balling his fists. George First jumped in front of Bill and Nigrim still wearing his mask, and growling. The troll stopped again, blinking.

"Plan B, Bill!" George shouted. "Go to the next underground entrance."

"But that way is longer and more dangerous," Bill

protested.

"No choice," Nigrim squeaked from the backpack.

"Go now, and take the injured man and the kids," George said. "I'll stay here and deal with the troll as long as I can, but I can't keep him confused for much longer."

"But what about you?"

"I'll get out of here once the group is safe. Go!"

"Imbecile troll!" Dr. Grout screamed. Each of his chins jiggled as he yelled. "I told you, it's just a mask!"

He let out an exasperated sigh, opened the book to a folded piece of paper stuck inside, and began reading aloud. Elise couldn't understand the words, but almost immediately, the hatch in the boiler room floor burst open from below.

Elise shrieked as a skeleton hand and arm emerged from the opening. "Stephen, get back!"

"Jeepers!" Stephen shouted as the rest of the skeleton climbed through the hatch.

The skeleton carried its skull in its hand and shambled with slow, herky-jerky steps over to Dr. Grout. The doctor continued to shout words Elise could not understand until a stream of colors began to emerge from the book.

It reminded her of the spell that had brought forth Mr. Gerald, the British soldier the day before. The colors moved like floating steam overhead, mixed, and then fell upon the skeleton's frame until it took the shape of a tall, thin man.

The head held in the man's hand had a narrow nose and small, close-set eyes. Long, stringy hair snaked down to where his shoulders would be. He wore white silk stockings, buckled leather shoes, knee-length pants, and the overcoat of an eighteenth-century gentleman.

Once the man was fully formed, he placed his head upon

his shoulders and twisted it into place. The head seemed wobbly but stayed attached once he removed his hands. Dr. Grout called out final words, closed the book, and pointed at Bill and the frozen kids.

The thin man turned toward them. In the hand where the head had been, he now carried what looked like a small pumpkin with flames licking its sides.

"Run!" George First screamed from behind his mask.

"Coop, Stephen, Elise, up the stairs! I'm right behind you!" Bill yelled.

Elise shoved Stephen ahead. "Go!" she yelled. Coop surged into view beside her. As they scrambled up the steps, she flung a glance over her shoulder to see George First still in a standoff with the troll. The thin man ignored the two of them, following Elise and the others with slow, choppy strides.

"Hurry!" Elise shouted.

The thin man jerked his arm up and threw the flaming pumpkin toward Elise. She leaped upward, taking the steps two at a time. Behind her, the pumpkin splatted the ground, shattering and releasing a ball of flame that scorched everything around it and almost lit her witch's cape on fire as it streamed behind her.

Elise stumbled trying to now jump up the steps three at a time. She righted herself and grabbed Mr. Hernandez's good arm, helping him through the lobby and outside of the school where Bill, Coop, and Stephen stood, panting.

"Who or what was that?" Coop asked, as they hurried down the sidewalk away from the building.

Bill wheezed, trying to catch his breath. "Believe it or not, I think that was Ichabod Crane."

TAYLOR PENSONEAU

CHAPTER ELEVEN

Aladdin's Castle

The group jogged down the block, frequently looking back to see if they were being followed. Mr. Hernandez limped between Elise and Coop, panting.

"Hey, guys, slow down," Elise said. "How are you doing, Mr. Hernandez?"

"I can go another block as far as Park Street," Mr. Hernandez huffed, holding his bent arm. "After that, I'm going to turn off and head to the hospital. We'll have to walk a little slower, though, if I'm going to keep up."

"There's a second entrance to the underground somewhere at the mall," Bill said as they all slowed down. He took off his backpack and unrolled the map.

"It's in the back corner of Aladdin's Castle arcade," Stephen said.

"How do you know that?" Bill asked, his eyebrows drawn together.

"I saw it on the map yesterday before you guys rolled it up." Stephen pulled his hand-drawn map from his backpack. "See?" He unfolded the piece of notebook paper. The map was crude but very similar to the one Bill held.

"OK," Bill said slowly, still staring at Stephen. "Let's head up Old Covered Bridge Road for a couple of blocks, and we'll hit the main mall entrance. I haven't been to the arcade in a while since I got my Atari, but you guys can help me find the underground entrance and then take off once I'm in."

"We can do that," Elise answered. Both Coop and Stephen nodded in agreement.

Elise helped Mr. Hernandez along as they began walking again.

"Mr. Hernandez?" Elise asked quietly.

"Yes?"

"Why were you at the school today?"

Bill turned to hear the answer.

"I—I knew I needed to protect you," he answered

"But how did you know to be at the school at noon today?" Stephen asked. "I mean, I'm glad you were there and all, but that sure was amazing timing."

"Because I heard Dr. Grout say that he had to stop the October Society from entering the underground today." Mr. Hernandez stopped walking and rubbed his arm. "He said the Society was planning to enter through the basement of the school and get the Cookbook back." He rubbed his arm again before continuing. "He said the children were going to guide the Society to the entrance at the school." Mr. Hernandez avoided eye contact with the group. "And I knew you were those children."

"Why were you talking with Dr. Grout?" Bill asked.

"Well . . . " Mr. Hernandez continued to look at the ground. "Because I was demanding that he return the Cookbook to me."

"To you? Do you mean to Ms. Hopper?" Elise asked. How had Mr. Hernandez known that Dr. Grout had it?

"No," Mr. Hernandez answered. "No, because I was the one who took the book from Ms. Hopper in the first place."

"What?" Elise cried. "It was you?"

"Yes."

"Who is this guy?" Bill asked.

"He owns the rest of the building where Ms. Hopper lives and has her bakery," Elise responded. "But why? Why would you do such a thing?" Tears stung at the corners of her eyes. Ms. Hopper trusted this kindly, helpful man, and all this time, he had been the cause of her troubles.

"I-I—" Mr. Hernandez stuttered before collecting himself. "Because I accepted Dr. Grout's offer to buy my part of the building. I wanted to retire and give the money to my kids." He finally looked up and met Elise's eyes. "But if Ms. Hopper doesn't sell her shop and the apartment, then there's no deal. Dr. Grout wants to tear down the whole block and build storage facilities, and that's the last holdup."

"But you said you didn't care about the money—that you didn't want to sell," Elise said.

"I'm sorry. I guess I lied because I didn't want to upset Ms. Hopper too much. But she's getting so old. She needs to retire, take a rest. I thought if I took the Cookbook away, she would forget her recipes and the shop would close down slowly making her have to sell. I gave the book to Dr. Grout.

He agreed to pay me extra for it."

"Not hurt her feelings!" Elise practically shouted. "You didn't think taking away her shop would hurt her feelings? It's all she has since her husband passed away."

"I know. Looking back, it doesn't seem like such a good idea." Mr. Hernandez absently jingled his key ring with his good arm. "I realized it was a bad plan when I saw Dr. Grout show up at the shop with that James man. A brute, he was! I didn't like the way he was trying to make Ms. Hopper leave right away. The guilt started getting to me."

"I bet it did!" Coop said.

"I said the same to Dr. Grout," Mr. Hernandez defended himself. "I told him he didn't have to threaten Ms. Hopper. The shop would be closing down soon enough. That's when he told me he had lost his patience." Mr. Hernandez shook his head.

"Talking to him last night, he said he'd learned that the October Society planned to go into the underground to get the book back and that you children were going to help find the entrance after school today. I knew you were in danger, and I had to do something to help make up for my mistake, and that's why I was at the school today."

"Wait a minute." The truth rolled through Elise's mind like a cold wave. "That's why you set up the interview with the newspaper's food critic. You knew Ms. Hopper would get a terrible review for everyone to see and the shop would close even quicker."

Mr. Hernandez just hung his head.

"Look!" Coop shouted before Mr. Hernandez responded. He was pointing back down the sidewalk.

The ghost of Ichabod Crane marched toward them,

holding another smoldering pumpkin. Drivers passing by seemed oblivious to the strange man shambling down the sidewalk.

"We need to move!" Bill shouted. "He can't match pace, but he'll keep coming. No more stopping until we get to the mall. I'll try and lure him underground and deal with him there."

The group began to run, but Mr. Hernandez quickly fell behind. Anger and empathy warred in Elise's mind. They had to hustle, but her mom would expect her to stay with him and help. She linked her arm though his good one as Coop helped on the other side. Ichabod continued his march, now just a hundred yards away.

"Come on!" Coop urged Mr. Hernandez, his voice high-pitched and panicky.

"I can't," Mr. Hernandez moaned. "You all go ahead. I'm just slowing you down." He looked at Elise. "You too. I'll head up Park Street to the hospital. It's only two more blocks. I'll see if I can get him to follow me. It's the least I can do."

Mr. Hernandez split off, cradling his arm as he cut across the street. Once on the other side, he paused and shouted at the lurching Ichabod. But although Ichabod was briefly distracted by Mr. Hernandez, he soon continued after the group.

"He didn't take the bait," Bill said. "Mr. Hernandez should be able to get to the hospital safely. Let's put some distance between us and Ichabod before we get to the mall."

༄

White Oaks Mall was busy even for a Friday. The group rode

the escalator up to the food court, which was scented with the mingled aromas of giant pretzels and cinnamon buns. Near the middle, they found an empty table where they could sit and plan.

"So according to the map, Aladdin's Castle contains an entrance to the underground," Bill said. "The arcade is on the lower level in the southeast hallway near the Sears anchor store. Once I find the entrance, there's an exit from the mall close by that you can use." Bill rolled up the map and poked Nigrim's head back into the backpack along with it.

"Yeah, you just pass Spencer's and Luca Pizza and then take a left," Stephen said. "Looks like the door to the underground is in the trolls' corner of the arcade. Bad luck for you, Bill." He shook his head.

"What does that mean?" Bill asked. "You don't mean real trolls?"

"No, that's what we call it because of the older boys who hang out there. Bunch of bullies. They don't let anyone else come back there. It's always dark, they sneak cigarettes, and man, do they smell." Stephen said.

"They smell just like James, Dr. Grout's troll," Elise said.

"Probably trolls in disguise," Bill responded.

"That would make sense." Elise nodded. She never would have realized that before. Of course, she never believed in trolls before.

"I may need you guys to provide a distraction while I slip past them to the entrance," Bill said.

"One thing before we go. Why Ichabod?" Coop asked.

"What do you mean?" Bill shouldered his pack and stuffed Nigrim's head back in again, eliciting a small squeak of complaint.

"He wasn't a bad guy in The Legend of Sleepy Hollow. Why does he seem so evil now?"

"I think he probably died badly at the hands of the headless horseman or he died lonely. Most likely he's still lingering as an angry spirit, so it's not hard for the November Men to summon him for their use."

"Huh," Coop said. "So, if it is Ichabod Crane, then why isn't he in Sleepy Hollow?"

"Long story short, when he disappeared after being chased by the Headless Horseman, there were rumors that he had survived the night and took up a new life two towns over, as in Legend Hollow. If that was the case, then it would make sense he would be buried here."

"Maybe." Coop didn't look totally convinced.

"My best guess," Bill said, tugging at the brim of his wizard's hat and pushing his chair in.

As the group approached the escalator, Coop grabbed Elise's arm.

"He's here! He's trying to come up the escalator!" He said pointing at Ichabod.

"He's having a tough time of it," Stephen pointed out as the gangly ghoul tried placing a foot on the moving stairs before drawing it back and then trying his other without success. Shoppers were lining up behind him, but he ignored them while grunting in frustration.

"Take the steps!" Bill shouted.

They turned and sprinted for the stairs, Elise's heart racing as fast as her feet. As they ran down the steps, Ichabod looked up from his struggles, and his eyes narrowed. The small pumpkin in his right hand began smoldering as he once again lurched toward the group.

"Spencer's is this way!" Stephen shouted. "Come on!"

They dashed along the lower level hall. Shoppers stopped in their tracks and stared, clearly startled at the sight of a witch, a clown, and a bearded man in a floppy wizard hat sprinting through the mall. Elise tossed a wild glance behind her. Ichabod raised the pumpkin but then lowered it. She thudded onward. Thank goodness—looked like Ichabod's throwing arm was a little out of practice.

Fountains, fake plants, and eventually Spencer's and Luca's Pizza flashed by as they ran. They all followed Stephen as he turned left down a hallway to the entrance of Aladdin's Castle.

The sounds of the arcade's games poured out of the doorway. Panting, they entered a dark, cavernous room smelling of teen boy body odor mixed with the liberal use of air freshener. Red carpet soiled from foot traffic covered the floor, and a low ceiling almost touched the tops of the games.

A row of pinball machines lined the wall to the right, teenagers hunched over them. Bells, bangs, and other sound effects filled the air creating a roar of sound that was almost disorienting. Rows of video game cabinets in the middle of the room emitted their own tidal wave of noise. A manager with slicked-back hair, cut-off jean shorts and a change belt roamed the room.

"That's troll's corner over there," Stephen said, pointing to a far corner where a seperate entrance made to look like a tunnel opened up into another black-lit room.

"Let's go," Bill said, leading the group toward the corner. They passed Centipede machines making dooom sounds, a Tron game playing its unique song, and a Pac-man machine rhythmically chomping pellets.

"Trolls!" Bill hissed, stopping short of the tunnel entrance.

A group of what appeared to be large older boys lurked in the dark tunnel around a Satan's Hollow game.

"Appropriate," Stephen said.

"Look, Jimmy Manx is with them," Coop pointed out.

"Figures," Elise said. "Probably too stupid to realize his buddies aren't even human."

Elise had seen the boys in the back room other times she had been at the arcade but for the first time, she realized how hulking they were. She even saw the end of a hairy tail peeking out of one their jeans legs. A spark of pity flared in her chest for Jimmy Manx. Poor guy—at least he'd found a peer group at his same mental level.

"So, they've been here the whole time, and they're just trolls in disguise?" Coop asked.

"Yes," Bill said. "OK, here's what we need to do. You kids distract the trolls, and I'll sneak into the underground entrance. I think I see it behind the Satan's Hollow game."

"How do we distract them?" Elise asked.

"I've got an idea. Follow me," Coop said. "Bill, get ready." Elise and Stephen followed him while Bill hid behind another machine near Troll's Corner.

"Hey! Hey!" Coop yelled from the entrance. The arcade manager stopped in his tracks, looking Coop up and down. Most of the players ignored the shouting, too engrossed in their games to look away. One of the trolls looked up from Satan's Hollow but only briefly, while Jimmy Manx turned and sneered.

"Hey, it's the Indian! The Indian bugbear!" he yelled before going back to his game.

"Wait—if he doesn't play D&D, how does he know about

bugbears?" Stephen asked.

"Let's worry about that later," Elise said. "I've got another idea. Be ready to run."

"Look!" she shouted, pointing down the hallway and waving her black witch's cape. "A fat kobold heading toward Luca's Pizza!"

All of the trolls now turned, glancing at Elise. The manager continued to look confused, and now some of the other arcade patrons were staring as well.

"Well, look at that," Elise shouted again while still pointing. "Is that a limping elf with the fat kobold?"

That was all the trolls could take. One of them with a blond mullet and an Incredible Hulk T-shirt led the others toward the arcade entrance.

Bill seized the moment and crawled on all fours into Troll's Corner toward Satan's Hollow. He was almost there when the last of the trolls noticed his wizard's hat scooting past.

"Hey!" the troll yelled, grabbing Bill by the ankle. "What you do?"

"Gah!" Bill exclaimed, now hanging upside down. His hat fell to the floor. Nigrim nearly spilled from the backpack, which fell from Bill's shoulder.

"Hey! You put him down this minute!" The arcade manager yelled.

The troll holding Bill reluctantly complied, seeing all of the attention in the arcade was now on him and his gang. Elise winced as he dropped Bill with a thud, still holding on to his ankle. Jimmy Manx looked up from his game, confused.

Coop quietly signaled the other kids to follow him. He used his foot to slide Bill's backpack over to himself. Once he had it, he began walking slowly toward the tunnel. Bill noticed and nodded at Coop.

"Now look, we've got a family arcade here," the manager scolded Bill and the trolls. "We don't stand for horseplay. You all cut it out right now, or you're eighty-sixed out of here for good. And that includes you, Jimmy Manx."

"What did I do?," Jimmy asked while pointing at himself.

Bill took the opportunity to place his hat back on his head. The trolls said nothing, looking at their feet and grunting instead of meeting the manager's eyes.

"Look at that!" yelled a boy. "Cool costume!"

Everyone swiveled their heads and looked at where he was pointing. Ichabod stood at the arcade entrance, holding a smoldering pumpkin.

"Oh, no!" Elise moaned.

The trolls gaped at the strange figure, ignoring Elise and the others now, but one of them still held Bill by the leg. He tried to shake loose while they were distracted but couldn't. He turned back to Elise, Coop, and Stephen.

"Go now and follow the map from the pack to find the book. After you get it, don't come back here. Exit through Hell's Gate in Washington Park."

"What about you?" Elise whispered back.

"Don't worry about me—go on your own. I've still got a trick or two up my sleeve. If you get into any danger, cut out and escape through Hell's Gate right away."

The troll holding Bill's ankle noticed the whispering and shook him.

"Now cut that out!" the manager yelled at the troll again. "I said no more horseplay."

The troll stopped shaking Bill and turned his attention back to Ichabod, who was now shambling awkwardly toward the group.

"Hey!" the manager said. "Get out here. You can't smoke in here."

"Come on," Elise said, grabbing Stephen by the shoulder.

The three of them snuck into Troll's Corner unnoticed. Sure enough, behind the Satan's Hollow game stood a door painted the same black color as the wall, making it nearly invisible unless you stood right by it.

"Should we go?" Coop asked, looking at the door and then at Elise. His eyes were wide.

Elise glanced at Bill, who was back on his feet between the arcade manager and the trolls. Bill removed his hat and withdrew something from inside that he threw toward Ichabod. It happened so fast she couldn't make out what it was. The object landed at Ichabod's feet, releasing a flash of light and smoke.

"Yes!" Elise grabbed the black handle and cracked open the door. "Hopefully, Bill can handle Ichabod and the trolls on his own."

"He's the best dungeon master around. If he can't handle them, nobody can," Stephen said.

A draft of air was the only indicator that the blackness beyond wasn't just a solid wall. Elise reached blindly in front of herself for anything to hold on to as they entered the space. As soon as they were inside, the door slammed shut, leaving them engulfed in darkness with the arcade sounds suddenly miles away.

CHAPTER TWELVE

Into the Tunnels

"Be still, everyone," Nigrim squeaked from the backpack.

He pulled his firework spark lantern from the pack, lighting up their surroundings. They were standing on a small platform leading to a long flight of stairs descending into darkness.

"I can't believe we're doing this," Coop whispered to the other lit-up faces.

"The adults said we weren't supposed to," Stephen said, his voice wavering.

"I know, but right now, we're the only ones who can go after the Cookbook and bring it back to Ms. Hopper," Elise said.

"And the Society needs it before Halloween and the jamboree," Coop added.

"Let's take a vote," Elise said. "Whoever thinks we should go after the book raise their hand."

She raised her own hand. Nigrim's small hand shot up, followed by Coop's. Stephen looked at the others, shrugged his shoulders, and then raised his hand.

"OK, it looks like we're going." Relief flooded Elise's body even as fear hovered in the background. "Stephen, Mom would kill me if she knew I was doing this, let alone taking you with me. You have to promise to stay near me so I can keep you safe."

"Yes, ma'am!" Stephen responded, rolling his eyes.

"OK, the clown suit doesn't help with the sarcasm, but I'll take it. Coop, grab the map out of the pack, and let's see where we're going. Let's make it quick in case the trolls figure out where we went."

Coop spread out the map on the floor near Nigrim's lantern.

"Here," Stephen said, tapping a large room halfway across the map. "This is where the Society said the Goblin Market was and where Dr. Grout stashed the book."

Coop drew a line along various tunnels from the Goblin Market back to the mall.

"Looks like it's about two miles. We need to head down these steps to what the map says is . . " Coop squinted to read the small print. "The trolley station, I believe it says."

"Trolley?" Stephen asked.

"Yeah, Legend Hollow had an urban trolley running through town until about forty years ago. This must have been one of the underground stations where the line originated and people could buy tickets and get on or off and stuff. I think some of the tracks would run along old coal mine shafts until they emerged above ground."

"Cool," Stephen said, nodding.

"Looks like we go through the abandoned station and then follow the rail line to the right," Coop said, tracing the path on the map with his finger. "Then we would connect to what looks like an underground drainage tunnel, go down that for a while before taking another right at an old mine shaft, then another right, and that would take us into the Goblin Market. Looks like a short tunnel shoots off to a doorway or something just before we get there. My guess is that's Hell's Gate."

"That's how we get out, Bill said." Elise responded. The image of enraged trolls and goblins filled her mind.

"Bill said it's supposedly guarded only from the outside. If we can't find it, then I guess we come back the same way we came in. Just trace our path back to here. Hopefully, by the time we would get back to the arcade, the trolls would have forgotten about all of the commotion and we could slip by them if they were still there."

"Hope we don't see those trolls again in the tunnels," Stephen said, looking back at the door.

"Will soon if don't move," Nigrim squeaked.

Coop rolled up the map and put it in the backpack. "OK, let's get going. I'll lead, and Nigrim can light the way."

Coop slung the pack over his shoulder with Nigrim perched atop, his spark casting light several feet in front of them. Coop began cautiously descending the steps with Stephen following behind. Elise brought up the rear with the darkness seeming to press against her back as they descended.

The steps were in good condition. Mall maintenance staff? It took nearly a minute of descending before they reached the bottom where the lantern revealed a large, rectangular room that smelled of mold and dust.

Yellow caution tape hung limply across the end of the stairs. The walls' dirty cream-colored tiles had been spray-painted with illegible words. Elise followed the others, stepping over the yellow tape onto a cracked concrete floor. Piles of rocks and plaster lay scattered about from where the ceiling had begun to cave in.

Rusted train tracks ran the length of the room, beginning at a boarded-up tunnel entrance on the left and exiting to the right through another tunnel where the boards had been torn away. Fading ornate letters painted on the opposite wall read dubois station, barely visible to Elise in the lantern light. It was also just bright enough to illuminate the worn and streaked clown makeup still adorning Stephen's face. Elise shuddered.

"What's that?" she asked, looking up at something dark in the ceiling.

"I'm not sure. Let's get closer." Coop walked forward until he stood under it. "It's a manhole, I think. The street is probably running right above us."

Beneath the manhole, a ragged sleeping bag was laid out on the floor along with an old radio, a lantern, a pile of clothes, and a box of Twinkies.

"Homeless people?" Elise asked,

"Probably," Coop responded.

"Geez, this place looks dangerous," Stephen said, peering through the darkness.

Elise nodded. "By the way, take off that clown wig, and throw it in your backpack with the clown shoes."

"Why?"

"It's distracting."

"Fine," Stephen said, taking off the wig and stuffing it away.

"That's our route over there," Coop said, pointing to the tunnel to the right. "Let's follow the tracks."

He led the group through the broken boards to the tunnel entrance. A dank, musty smell hit their noses as they walked in. They followed the tracks for about five minutes as the ground gradually rose toward the ceiling. That must be where the old trolley surfaced to street level, Elise thought. But the ceiling had long ago collapsed and buried the tracks forever underground.

Someone had dug a large hole to the right of the rubble pile. Inside, crude wooden steps led down into darkness.

"I think that's an old mining tunnel," Stephen said. "On the map, it went in the direction we want to go."

"Let me check," Coop said, taking the map out of his bag. Nigrim shone his light upon the unrolled paper.

"Yup, you're right," Coop said, tracing the tunnel line.

"I know," Stephen responded with annoying smugness.

Coop ignored Stephen. "Looks like we can follow this tunnel until we hit our next turn in about 200 yards."

Stephen folded his arms. "Like I said."

Elise nudged him. "He just needed to double check. Don't get so sensitive."

Nigrim's light revealed another tunnel at the bottom of the hole. Coop carefully slung his pack back on and descended the stairs with the rest of the group following. The tunnel ran in two directions: straight ahead and back in the direction they had come. They continued forward for another minute with the darkness almost swallowing the light emitted by the firework spark.

The darkness weighed upon Elise like some sort of shroud. How much longer? Should they turn back? Then suddenly the overbearing darkness began to lift. A faint light source came from the ceiling twenty yards ahead.

"Another manhole?" Stephen asked.

"Maybe. Let's go see," Elise said.

Stephen jogged ahead of the group toward the spot but suddenly began waving his arms wildly, crying out.

"Grab him!" Elise exclaimed.

Coop jumped forward as Stephen began to fall forward. He grabbed Stephen around the waist and yanked him backward, the two crashing to the ground.

Elise dashed over. "Are you alright?" she asked, helping the boys to their feet.

"I think so," Stephen said, brushing himself off.

"What happened?"

"There's a hole!" Stephen pointed at the spot where he had almost fallen.

"Look at that," Coop said, letting out a slow whistle. The lantern revealed a circular hole ten feet wide. Looking down into the darkness, Elise couldn't see the bottom.

"Looks like a sinkhole," Coop said.

He picked up a small rock and tossed it in. The rock clanked as it hit the wall, then clinked a few more times as it continued downward. Each time, the sound was fainter and fainter until finally the rock landed with a splash somewhere a long way down.

"Stephen, don't get ahead of Coop again," Elise said shakily, grabbing her brother's arm.

"Sorry. I was just checking out the light."

Elise had forgotten about the light above in all of the excitement. Narrow rays of light came from a hole high in the ceiling.

"Probably an airhole for the miners who used to work down here," Coop said, wiping sweat from his forehead.

"It is, yes," Nigrim squeaked. "Elves, dwarfs add to their tunnels to."

"So, where do we go from here?" Coop asked, looking about.

Nigrim held his firework spark up to his face and whispered a command that caused it to brighten.

"Well, isn't that something," Stephen said. "It obeys commands like a pet!"

"Maybe we should have done that a little earlier." Elise said.

"Can't do it for long. Can burn out." Nigrim responded.

The brighter light illuminated two rough openings in the rock walls, which looked as if they were entrances into additional tunnels.

Elise and the others poked their heads in and found what appeared to be relatively modern construction with smooth concrete lining the walls, ceilings, and floor.

"Maybe I read the map wrong," Coop said, confusion creasing his face.

"To the right is a sewer tunnel, and to the left is a storm drain tunnel," Stephen announced without asking to see the map.

"Which one do we take?" Elise asked.

"To the left—the storm drain," Stephen responded confidently.

Whew! "Good," Elise said. "I didn't like the idea of

stomping off into a bunch of sewage."

"You sure, Stephen?" Coop asked.

"It's the route you traced on the map. I'm sure," Stephen said.

"If he says he's sure, then he's sure," Elise said. Her little brother might be smug about his amazing memory, but it was usually right.

"To the left it is," Coop said, leading the group into the drainage tunnel.

The tunnel ran in what Elise guessed to be a north-south direction. A trail of water trickled over green algae through a four-foot-wide channel in the middle. On either side of the channel ran narrow concrete walkways two feet above the water. The ceiling was so low that they could barely stand up straight. Coop chose the walkway on the right of the tunnel, and they walked single file in the opposite direction of the flowing water.

As they followed the tunnel south, they passed several small drains in the walls that emitted more trickles of water into the main channel. The tunnel slowly curved one way and then the other. They trudged along for a few minutes until Coop held up his hand, halting them.

Elise peered around him. Was that a pile of clothes up ahead on the path? Coop signaled for the group to step down from the path. Elise did as ordered, her shoes squelched in the cold water.

Coop skirted around the clothing pile, and as Elise passed by, a sudden snort made her jump. The pile of clothes was actually a man who was sleeping and snoring softly. His clothes were filthy and torn in spots. Did the items in the trolley station belong to him?

Stephen paused by the man, looking into his bearded face. Elise grabbed his shoulder, attempting to pull him along, but he shook himself free. He took off his backpack and began searching through it.

"Come on, Stephen!" Elise hissed.

Stephen signaled "one second" with his finger. He then pulled a bright red apple from his pack and set it next to the man before sloshing back to the group. Elise flushed when she realized why he ad paused.

They continued in silence, the squishing of their soaked shoes the only sound above the now rising water. Elise noticed that as the water began to flow faster debris began floating by. The occasional water-logged cardboard box and random single shoes bobbed and even a small rusted kid's wagon was pulled along in the current. Even more random discarded objects were deposited by the waters on the on the walkways making it necessary to step over them.

"It's probably raining up top," Coop said, seeming to read Elise's thoughts. "Let's hurry up before this storm drain and path become flooded."

They increased to nearly a jogging pace while they kept their eyes on the rising water.

"Stop!" Nigrim suddenly peeped.

Coop halted so sharply that Stephen ran into his back and Elise into Stephen's. "Oof!"

"Goblins, I smell," Nigrim said, sniffing at the air.

Elise's heart began to race.

"Do we run?" Stephen asked, his voice high.

"Too late. Not discover us yet, but they getting close. Need to hide," Nigrim said, scanning the ceiling and walls. "There!" He pointed to an overhang where the wall met the ceiling above the path. "Crawl up. Hide until pass."

They wasted no time grabbing at the overhang. Coop was able to secure a hold on the ledge first and pulled himself up. Lying flat, he then helped pull up Stephen and Elise. Grime and spider webs plastered their faces as they found their hiding places.

Nigrim closed the lantern and hid it in the backpack along with himself. The others lay as still and flat as they could while trying to keep their breathing as quiet as possible.

It wasn't long before the first pitter-patter of goblins' feet came trotting along the very path they had been traveling. Elise dared to open one eye. There were three of them, followed closely by a filthy opossum. They carried a small light of their own that emit a small glow before them and cast shadows on the walls.

They made short grunting sounds and high-pitched noises that reminded Elise of whining dogs. Were they talking to each other?

They were the same height as kobolds but skinnier, wearing no shoes and barely enough clothing to cover their dark green and brown skin. What she could see of their heads and bodies appeared hairless. Each had a small bag tied to its waist or hanging from a strap across its shoulders, and they carried small knives and clubs. Elise squeezed both eyes shut and held her breath.

They passed the group in their hiding spot, continuing their strange conversation. Elise breathed deeply, opening her eyes again, but her relief quickly faded when one of the goblins stopped grunting and cast its light toward the ledge above.

"Grunt, grunt, wee. I smell you, do you smell me?" it said,

TAYLOR PENSONEAU

sniffing at the air.

The other goblins were now sniffing too and looking about the tunnel. Elise grabbed both Coop's and Stephen's hands, squeezing them tight. Both of the boys squeezed back.

"See!" a goblin shouted, pointing at the ledge.

All three goblins ran over. The first stood at the base of the wall and raised its hands while the second climbed onto its shoulders. Elise lay petrified as the third goblin began climbing the others with the opossum on its shoulders.

She let out a scream as the goblin's hairless head appeared above the ledge. Its eyes glared into hers, yellow and cold. A knife swung toward her, just missing her shoulder.

"Get away!" Elise scrambled up, banging her head on the concrete ceiling above her. Youch! Woozily, she kicked out toward the menacing creature but missed.

The goblin smiled, showing ragged yellow teeth. "What you have for me?" it asked, raising its knife to strike again.

"Ahh!" Coop yelled wordlessly, and pushed past Elise to kick at the goblin's head. He made contact with a loud crack. It swayed back and forth, and the opossum fell from its shoulder bouncing into the water. The opossum squealed as it was swept away. The goblin steadied itself on the shoulders of the goblin below, gripping the concrete ledge. It blinked its eyes and shook its head, then once again the terrible smile split its green face as it let out a piercing yell.

"Squee!" the other two goblins shrieked, joining his battle cry.

"Go away!" Elise shouted, kicking at the leering face missing again.

Light glinted menacingly off the shiny knife in the goblin's hand as it moved about inches from her.

"Hey!" A deep voice boomed from somewhere in the tunnel. The beam of a flashlight bounced toward them.

"Eeek!" the top goblin screamed, and jumped from the shoulders of the one below him.

Elise trembled as the goblins retreated. And now who was coming at them?

The three goblins stood shoulder to shoulder, knives drawn and pointed toward the approaching light.

Elise rolled to the edge, and Coop and Stephen slid next to her, panting heavily as she squinted down. It was the man they'd seen sleeping on the path. He clutched a flashlight in one hand and what appeared to be a short shovel in the other. His large boots made a rubbery, clomping sound as he rushed toward the goblins.

The creatures let out another high-pitched squeal and charged toward the man, but he swung the shovel, knocking the closest goblin into the others causing all three to fall into the water like screeching bowling pins.

No sooner did the goblins plunge into the rising water than they were pulled helplessly downstream. In moments, the squealing, flailing troop vanished, swallowed by the darkness.

"You all right?" the bearded man said in a gruff voice.

"Yes, sir," Elise answered, blinking into the light the man held aloft in his left hand.

"Well, let me help you down, then." He grabbed Elise's hand, helping her off the ledge and back down to the concrete walkway, then doing the same for Coop and Stephen.

"Not sure what the three of you are doing down here, but I'm glad I came along," the man said, taking an apple from his pocket. He took a bite, winking at Stephen. Stephen smiled back.

"The goblins will probably manage to drag themselves out of that water in five or ten minutes, so I recommend you best skedaddle out of here before they return." He crunched into the apple again, chewed, and swallowed. "This tunnel goes for another couple of minutes before it hits an old mining tunnel that splits off to the right." He wiped at his mouth with the back of his hand. "You need to take that split to the right. It goes to Hell's Gate, and you can run through it into Washington Park."

"We can't do that, sir," Elise said.

"Why not?" The bearded man did not appear to like Elise's response.

"We need to go to the Goblin Market to get back something that was stolen."

"I see." The man rubbed his long, grey-streaked beard. "Well, I don't recommend it, and these waters are only going to keep rising until this tunnel is full." He took a final bite of the apple and tossed it into the water. "If you must, then I'll do what I can to delay the goblin folk that I dunked." He looked back over his shoulder. "Head up this path about another minute or so. You'll see a tunnel turn off to the right. If you follow that for another five, ten minutes, you'll hit the Goblin Market. The path to Hell's Gate splits off about halfway in case you decide to change your mind."

Elise's heartbeat had almost returned to normal. "Thank you, sir, and thank you for helping us with the goblins."

The man nodded his head, turned in the opposite direction, and sloshed away. Only the dim glow of his flashlight showed that he had ever been there, and soon even that disappeared into the darkness.

CHAPTER THIRTEEN

To Summon a Ghost

"Come on," Coop said.

The group followed the man's directions, keeping an eye on the rising water and walking as fast as they could. The roar of the increasing rapids made conversation nearly impossible.

Just as the man had said and as the map indicated, soon after taking a right turn they came upon another tunnel that split off further to the right. Elise peered in and saw slats of light piercing an iron grate at the end of it. The light revealed a rocky pathway but no water, goblins, or trolls to Elise's relief.

"Hell's Gate," Stephen said over the sound of the rushing water.

"I think so," Coop yelled back.

"Let's keep moving," Elise said.

"I hope we find this Goblin Market soon. We might run

out of pathway if this water keeps rising," Coop shouted.

The water was now coming up over the path in places. Elise stepped carefully. She was bordering on panic until she noticed a brighter light about a hundred yards ahead.

"Is that it? Is that the market?" Coop pointed at the glow, which revealed an opening in the tunnel.

A large structure straddled the width of the storm drain with rough stone steps leading up to it from the path. Elise thought she heard the strains of singing or chanting rising above the sounds of the water.

"Must be," Nigrim squeaked loudly from the top of the backpack.

They were almost there. "Hold down the chatter, everybody. Once we get closer, we can take a peek inside," Elise said.

Everyone moved in silence until Coop raised his hand for them to halt just feet from the steps to the entrance. "There's more debris blocking the path in front of the stairs. Looks like an old box spring mattress."

Together they leaned it against the wall, clearing the way.

"I guess somebody was sleeping on it all the way down here," Stephen said. "I would hate to think what that would be like." He shivered.

"Nigrim, do you think you can get inside the market and scout it out without being seen?" Coop asked the tiny creature.

"Yes," he piped back without hesitation.

"Good. That ghost soldier can help us grab the book, but first, we need to know what's going on in there." Elise patted Nigrim lightly on the head. "Be careful."

Elise looked up to the top of the stairs. The chanting and

shrieks only seemed to be getting louder.

"If you're in any danger or you think you might be discovered, get out of there right away, OK?" she pleaded with the small elf. "We'll escape back the way we came in."

Nigrim nodded his tiny head and climbed down the backpack and Coop's legs before handing his firework spark to Elise. He then made his way up the stone steps and peered into the market entrance before slipping inside.

Nigrim's firework brought Elise little comfort as doubt began to crawl into her mind. Should she have pursued the Cookbook and put all the others at risk? Coop would probably rather be at home reading a book, and Stephen should be sitting safely in the kitchen practicing his violin. And then there was poor Nigrim. The little elf was now far from his hole in the wall of the Plumber's shop, facing the market's dangers all by himself. No way her mother and Ms. Hopper would have approved of them being down here either. Guilt gnawed at her. What if something terrible happened to them, and she and Stephen never made it home? How could her mother deal with having them vanish just like Dad?

Several long, agonizing minutes passed before Nigrim once more appeared at the opening. He snuck as quietly as a cat to the group, who now stood in an inch of water covering the path.

"What did you see?" Coop asked, scooping Nigrim up.

"Oh, my," he squeaked. "Gathering!"

"A gathering? What kind of gathering?"

"Of witches, bad witches. Sabbatical. Witches' sabbatical!" Nigrim babbled.

"What's a witches' sabbatical?" Stephen asked.

"Leader of coven call witches to gather," Nigrim answered.

"How many were there?" Elise asked.

"Couple so far." Nigrim looked back over his shoulder toward the Goblin Market before continuing. "Goblins, trolls, witches, and spirits there were. Dancing, chanting, and swirling around a big fire." He flapped his hands above his head for emphasis.

Elise saw fear in his eyes. "How were the witches dressed?" Elise asked.

"Um." Nigrim rubbed his chin. "Ragged robes, long dresses."

"Hmm," Elise said. "And the spirits?"

"All kinds. Some white, some see-through." His eyes widened. "Some with no faces at all." Nigrim shivered. "Not want to see them again."

"I understand, and we won't ask you to go back in," Elise reassured him.

"I—I can do. Have some fairy dust, and—" Nigrim held aloft a small cloth pouch from his pocket.

"No, it's OK. You've done enough," Coop said.

"He's right," Elise agreed. "Just one more question. Did you see a large book?"

"Yes, just like soldier say. In corner. On a stand ten elves tall. Behind a pile of shiny things. Couldn't see cover."

"That has to be it," Coop said. "How many goblins?"

"Many. Some playing with their shiny things, some sing, some dance." He did a little dance to imitate them. "Some in their animal form."

"Animal form?" Coop asked.

"Yes, like opossum saw earlier with goblins. They can change. They can hide." Now Nigrim hunched and scooted about. "Look like cats or dogs, even. Seen them in streets before, have I."

"What are goblins afraid of?" Elise asked.

"Well," Nigrim scratched at his chin again while thinking. "Daylight. Any bright light. "

"We could use that," Elise said, nodding toward the firework lantern.

"Also, scared of horses, yes, scared of horses too. Worry about getting stepped on. Oh, and witchcraft. It scare them."

"You would think that they wouldn't want to hang out around with witches in there then," Stephen said.

"No. But they will serve a master." Nigrim nodded his head and crossed his arms "Out of fear. Or they're given shiny things maybe."

"Here's what we'll do." As everyone turned to her, Elise pulled her witch hat and shoes from her backpack and began getting dressed.

Coop huffed in surprise. "Elise, you're not thinking—"

She cut him off. "It sounds like a pretty crazy scene in there, so I'm going to try and use all that commotion to my advantage. Walk in casual—you know, just another witch, and if that works, I'll try and blend into the background and sneak into the corner to grab the book from the pedestal."

"I'm not sure they're going to buy you being a witch," Stephen said quietly.

"They might if I can bring my own ghost with me," Elise said with a grin. "I think now is a good time to summon Mr. Gerald. Coop, give me the book on the War of 1812 from Bill's backpack."

Coop dug through the pack and produced the book. She opened to the page with the painting of the marching British soldiers.

"Now what was the phrase Ms. Hopper used when she summoned Mr. Gerald from the page?" She waved her hand around above the book. "Hocus pocus, come out!"

Nothing happened except for the sound of Stephen laughing above the noise of the water.

"That's not it, Elise. Not even close."

Elise rolled her eyes. "OK, fine, then. What was it?"

"Let me see." Stephen was quiet for a moment before looking down at the page. "I think it was . . . " He waved his hand. "Hidey ho, you are released from below, Mr. Gerald. Please come forth from the page."

Nothing.

"Hmm, I thought that was it. Maybe my memory has finally failed me."

"Let me try." Elise took the book and swished her hand above it, chanting the same words Stephen had used.

Suddenly a swirl of colors began floating from the page until Mr. Gerald stood before them once more, holding his ancient musket. He patted at the dried blood on his jacket while looking about the tunnel.

"Wow!" Stephen exclaimed, looking at Elise with raised eyebrows. Coop stared at her too.

She'd done it! But . . . how?

"I'm down below in the tunnels again, I see," Mr. Gerald said, snapping to attention.

"Yes, you are, Mr. Gerald," Elise said. "Welcome back."

"Was it you who summoned me this time?"

"Yes. Um, I hope that's okay."

"A proper witch, I see." Mr. Gerald nodded approvingly.

"Me? No, not really." Elise glanced at Coop and Stephen, who were both still staring at her. "We need your help. We're back at the Goblin Market where you found yourself the other day, and we were hoping that you could guide us to the book. The one that you saw on the pedestal. Then we can leave, and we'll release you back to your grave."

"Fair enough." Mr. Gerald gave Elise a brief salute.

"Guide me once we get in there, but try not to be too obvious about it."

"A bit of skullduggery, then," Mr. Gerald said with a wink.

"You're not going in there without me, Elise," Coop said, stepping forward.

"I'll be OK." She said trying to sound confident.

"Maybe, but I'm still not letting you go in with just one ghost. No offense, Mr. Gerald."

"None taken."

"I'll try and blend into the jamboree. If you need help, I'll be there." Coop dug through his backpack and produced his white sheet with eye holes.

"I'm not sure how convincing that is," Elise said. "Everyone has seen that costume before."

"It'll be new to the goblins. Hopefully, it'll trick or at least confuse them for a little while."

"Yes, yes," Nigrim said, nodding his head.

"Well . . . " It did feel good knowing that Coop would be in the room with her. "OK. Stephen, you stay with Nigrim, and have the light ready to lead us out when we return."

TAYLOR PENSONEAU

CHAPTER FOURTEEN

The Goblin Market

Elise and her two ghosts entered a room engulfed in a kind of chaos that she had never seen before. In the middle of the room, witches swayed before a bonfire that burned so hot she thought it might singe her wig and hat. Several shrieking, nearly transparent, spirits swirled above the flames while goblins and trolls danced and sang at its edges.

More goblins were drinking from jugs and wrestling with each other among piles of shiny metal and trinkets. Nearly reaching the ceiling, the mounds contained coins, silverware, cups, cans, trash, and anything else that would attract the eye of simple-minded, mischievous creatures.

Uh oh. Elise was alarmed that none of the witches were dressed like a traditional witch like her, as Stephen had warned. None were the kind from Halloween ads or like the ones she saw on TV. Instead, they were clothed in tattered robes, old dresses with funny hats, or in some cases—Elise blinked—no clothes at all. Luckily, they appeared to be so lost in their chanting and ritual that they took no notice of her and the other two figures sneaking among the piles of goblin riches.

On the map, this room was labeled as the storage area for the trolley line cars, but the goblins and trolls had expanded it. Rough stairs had been dug out of a rock wall, ascending to another room that she couldn't see clearly.

"Only a few witches are here so far," Coop hissed above the noise. "The rest must still be gathering."

Elise nodded, then put her finger to her lips as a goblin scampered by. It climbed up a mountain of tin cups, lunch boxes, and garage tools. An opossum and a small dog chased it, both giggling and singing nonsensical songs.

"Mr. Gerald," Elise whispered once the goblins had passed. "Where was the pedestal with the book?"

"It was back there, behind that second pile to the left." He pointed toward the far corner of the room.

Elise nodded and made her way around a mountain of old teapots and silverware to discover another mountain of junk. It teetered next to what looked like the reading stand in the school library.

On it lay a large book with a black cover. Ms. Hopper's Cookbook! Elation shot through her—they'd found it! She considered doing a little dance of delight but caught herself.

Just then, two goblins wrestling near the pedestal jostled the junk pile. A goblin with brown skin finally gained the advantage and pinned the other to the ground, squealing in victory. It looked around to see who had noticed its victory before it rested its eyes on the new witch with the ghosts in tow.

"Scree!" it hissed from its perch atop the other goblin, and pointed at Elise.

Her heart began to pound. "Coop, get the book but do it slowly. Mr. Gerald and I will try to deal with these goblins," Elise whispered. He nodded under his bed sheet.

"What shall I do, ma'am?" Gerald stood at the ready as the goblins drew near.

"I—I'm, not sure," Elise said. "Just, um, just go behind that tippy-looking pile and be ready to shoot that musket or cause a commotion if I nod to you."

"Yes, ma'am." Gerald saluted and marched off past the wary goblins.

"You witch?" the brown goblin squealed at Elise.

Elise's throat was so tight that she couldn't immediately speak.

"I say, you witch?" the brown goblin asked again, sticking a jagged fingernail in her face. "Mister Dr. Grout say to watch out for October people."

"They do sneaky sneaky." The green goblin added.

"Y-yes." Elise gulped. "I'm a witch. Abracadabra." She waved her hand in front of her. "See?"

"Just a girl," the brown goblin hissed at the green goblin.

"Look." The green goblin pointed at the pedestal. Elise glanced over her shoulder and saw Coop tucking the large book under his bed sheet.

"October Society!" the brown goblin shouted in a piercing voice. It tensed its body, ready to spring.

"Gerald!" Elise shouted, jumping away from the goblins. The nearby pile teetered back and forth twice before crashing down on the goblins, drowning out their screams. The chanting and singing in the room fell silent.

"Run!" Elise shouted, and sprinted for the door.

Coop and Mr. Gerald dashed after her but several trolls were now lumbering toward them. The witches stood frozen, watching them with unblinking eyes, while spirits screamed and raged above the fire. None other than Dr. Grout himself came trotting out of the room that overlooked the proceedings below.

"What is happening?" He stopped cold when he spotted Elise. "Stop them immediately! I warned you to be on alert for the October Society" he shouted, pointing at the group now in full flight. "Bring them to me along with the book! Goblins! Trolls! Spirits, Witches! Do your worst!"

Elise pounded for the exit, her breath coming in short, hard gasps. The trolls were gaining on them! Even more terrifying, the witches had begun chanting anew with several gesturing gnarled hands or balled fists in their direction.

A witch with long grey hair and a tattered robe shouted and waved her hands as the spirits above the fire moved in unison with her motions. They spun in tighter and tighter circles about the witch until she spoke a final word. They turned their terrifying faces toward Elise while letting out blood-curdling howls.

Elise shrieked as the ghosts began to swarm toward her, but at that moment a large fireball exploded from the bonfire. The grey witch collapsed, the ghosts scattered and the trolls and goblins cowered.

Little Nigrim came running from the fire, clutching his fairy dust pouch, and scurried past Elise out the entrance.

"Run! Don't waste the chance he's given you!" Mr. Gerald

shouted, putting his arms around Elise and Coop and pushing them toward the exit.

A grey goblin and a ragged-looking dog had gathered their wits and were charging forward to cut off their escape. Elise stumbled as the goblin drew a rusted knife from its belt while the dog snarled and snapped.

Mr. Gerald took his musket in both hands, ready to swing it as a club. Before he could use it, the grey goblin tumbled to the ground, landing on its face and letting out a muffled scream. Behind it stood Stephen, his hands still out after shoving it. The dog spun on Stephen but yelped and scampered away when it saw his face covered in the grotesquely smeared clown makeup.

A troll that had drawn near stopped to stare at Stephen as well, and that was all the opening Mr. Gerald needed. He swung the butt end of his musket and connected with the troll's head with a loud *crack*.

The troll was stunned by the blow, but the goblins had gotten over the shock of the fireball and were swarming toward them from all corners of the room. They ran through the entrance to the top of the stairs where Nigrim stood, holding his firework lamp.

Coop threw off his sheet, stuffed the Cookbook into his pack, and yanked it over his shoulders.

"Hurry, Coop!" Elise implored.

The light from the lantern bounced about the tunnel as they bounded down the long steps. Screaming goblins and trolls closed in from behind.

"Oh no, the path is completely flooded!" Stephen yelled.

"What do we do? Swim?" Elise shouted to Coop.

"No," Coop said, grabbing the dirty box spring mattress.

"We float."

Mr. Gerald grabbed a section of the mattress and held it just above the rapids. He looked back at the trolls and goblins now only steps behind. "Get on and I'll hold it. I'll get on last."

"It can't float all of us," Stephen yelled.

"Just grab on to the front, and we'll use it like a life preserver," Elise said. "Coop, make sure you keep the pack out of the water so the book doesn't get wet and don't drown Nigrim!"

"Go!" Mr. Gerald yelled as a large troll with a long red beard grabbed his musket.

He lost his grip on the mattress as the children jumped on. The mattress wobbled as the back half sank under their weight, submerging their legs, but the front end stayed afloat. It soon began drifting downstream, leaving Mr. Gerald behind.

"I'll slow them down!" Mr. Gerald yelled, wrestling the red-bearded troll to the ground and taking back his musket. He smashed it into the troll's face, but this only seemed to enrage the troll further.

Several goblins slid beyond Gerald to the bottom step. They eyed the fast-moving current nervously.

"See!" Nigrim screamed from atop Coop's pack. "I tell you. Can't swim!"

Another large troll grabbed two nearby goblins and tossed them at the makeshift raft. The first splashed nearby and sank immediately. The second goblin was better aimed, and bounced off the mattress, nearly knocking Stephen into the water before sliding off itself, screaming as it flailed and sank. The impact made Coop lose his grip on the wet mattress, and he began to slide toward the submerged end.

"Help me!" Stephen screamed, grabbing one of Coop's backpack straps.

Elise grabbed Coop's arm, and they strained to keep Coop's pack and head above the water. As Coop grabbed at the slick surface, they hauled him back up.

"Thanks," Coop panted.

The troll looked about for more goblin projectiles, but the mattress had floated out of reach before he could snag another to throw. The troll snorted with frustration and jumped into the water, briefly disappearing before reemerging. He stood waist deep in the water, struggling to keep his footing on the slick bottom as thousands of gallons of water pushed against his legs. Eventually, the troll steadied itself, plodding after them.

"Kick your legs!" Coop shouted. "We've got to get this thing moving faster."

They kicked as hard as they could while the troll roared in fury. Elise looked back and saw a stick floating on the rapids toward them. Wait—that wasn't a stick. It was Mr. Gerald's musket! And trailing behind it was Mr. Gerald himself, floating face down.

"Oh, no—poor Mr. Gerald!" Elise moaned.

The boys hung their heads at the sight. As the body came alongside, it bumped the mattress near Stephen. Mr. Gerald's head popped up from the water.

"Aaah!" Stephen yelled.

"There you are," the soldier said, water pouring from his mouth. "Never was a great swimmer."

"We thought you had drowned," Elise cried.

"Can't. Already dead." Mr. Gerald smiled.

"I'm glad you're . . . well?" Coop said. "Or at least as well as you can be, being dead and all."

"The turnoff to the Devil's Gate opening is coming up," Stephen said, pointing ahead.

"How are we going jump off and get to that tunnel without getting dunked?" Elise asked. "If we slow down too much, that troll is going to catch up."

"Someone hold raft while others get off," Nigrim squeaked.

"I can do it," Mr. Gerald volunteered.

"But you'll never be able to get away from that troll if you stay and hold the mattress," Stephen said, doubling up his grip on the front of the raft.

"I'll be fine. I'll stop that brute and allow the lot of you to escape. Afterward, you can bind me back to the book and let me go at my grave."

"We will." At least, Elise hoped so. She tried to sound confident.

"All right, that's sorted. We're almost there." Mr. Gerald released one hand from the mattress and grabbed the edge of the tunnel. He submerged briefly, but his hand still grasped the mattress edge, holding fast until he reemerged. He managed to climb onto the dry path and pull the front of the mattress up behind him.

"Here comes the troll!" Coop yelled.

Elise's blood seemed to freeze as the large troll continued its slow but steady march through the water, all the while roaring angry, unintelligible words at them.

"Go, go!" she yelled.

Stephen clambered up the mattress to the safety of the path, followed by Elise. Coop was last, moving cautiously to protect both Nigrim and the backpack from the water. He crawled up the wobbly mattress, reaching the path just as the troll grabbed at his ankle.

"No!" Elise screamed.

The creature missed but snagged a corner of the mattress, ripping it from Mr. Gerald's grasp.

"Run, young ones! I'll hold him off!" Mr. Gerald jumped back into the water, landing on the troll. The monster lost its balance in the fast-flowing stream. As it slipped below the surface, it lashed out wildly and managed to get a handful of Mr. Gerald's uniform, taking them both below.

"The 1812 book! Give it to me now!" Elise shouted at Coop, who lay panting on the path.

Coop slung the pack off his shoulders, and Stephen yanked out the book. He handed it to Elise as Mr. Gerald and the troll burst up out of the water. The troll was attempting to climb over the old soldier so that it could get to the path and its prey.

Elise flipped desperately through the book to the picture of British soldiers and began waving her hands and chanting, "Hidey ho, you are released from below, Mr. Gerald. Please come forth from the page."

Nothing happened. The troll continuing climbing up Mr. Gerald, using him for traction against the torrent of water.

"That's wrong—that's the summoning spell!" Coop shouted, rising to his feet. "Try something else—something that will bind him again."

"But we didn't hear the binding spell!" Panic fluttered in Elise's throat as the angry troll drew ever nearer.

"You're a witch. Just try something," Stephen said, putting his hand on her shoulder.

"But I'm not . . . " Elise's voice trailed off. She closed her eyes, blocking out the troll now just feet away, and began chanting.

"Mr. Gerald, you have gone to and fro, but now it's time for you to come out of that flow, to the page once more you go."

"It's working!" Stephen shouted. "I told you—you're a witch!"

Elise opened her eyes. Mr. Gerald was dissolving into a swirl of colors beneath the troll.

"What!" the Troll shouted, falling into the water with a great splash. He flailed his arms but could not right himself before being swept away.

Mr. Gerald swirled in the air above Elise, then swooped into the open book. Was that a wink he gave her before vanishing? Elise snapped the book shut, blinking. It had worked!

"That was something," Coop said, gently taking the book from her and securing it in the backpack.

"I . . . Let's talk about it later. We need to get out of here," Elise said, heading toward the end of the tunnel and Hell's Gate.

They gathered in front of the gate. Light from outside snuck through the bars, slashing the ground in straight lines. Coop put his hand on an old metal latch.

"On the count of three, I'll press the handle, and you guys push on the gate to open it. Then we'll run straight through. Just keep running and don't look back until we're out of the park. Got it?" Coop asked.

"Got it," Stephen answered as Elise nodded.

"OK, one, two, three." Coop yanked down on the handle, and it gave way with a loud click.

Elise and Stephen both put their hands on the gate and

pushed with all of their weight. It made a loud metal-on-metal screeching noise as it swung open.

The light was nearly blinding after so many hours in the darkness, and Elise shielded her eyes with one hand as she ran. Everything looked blurry. She weaved her way between trees, searching for a sidewalk or path to follow as Coop and Stephen ran beside her. A troll roared somewhere behind them, and remembering Coop's orders, she ran as hard as she could without looking back.

TAYLOR PENSONEAU

CHAPTER FIFTEEN

Halloween and the Jamboree

From the journal of Niles Folsom, High Doctor, October Society of
New York City

Commentary Regarding the Happenings of All Hallows Eve

Saturday, October 31, 1986, Legend Hollow, New York

*W*ith the unexpected aid of local children and a friendly
spirit, the Cookbook has been recovered and not a moment
too soon. The reckless actions of Dr. Grout and the November
Men have stirred up the shadow folk and, on this All Hollow's
Eve, weakened the barrier between this world and the next to the
point of tearing it asunder.

Without the Cookbook, Dr. Grout's power has been greatly
reduced, and he is on the run. George First has enlisted the aid
of local jogah, and he and the Plumber lie in wait to bring the

malcontent Dr. Grout before the October Society for punishment
and to end this sordid chapter once and for all.

Tonight, the Society will hold a jamboree in the Eastern Woods
near the old Polstein Cemetery, where numerous supernatural
happenings have been observed. They will monitor the barrier
between the two worlds and try to hold out against the many
things attempting to break through.

Costumed children swarmed the neighborhood. Squeals of
joy surrounded Elise, but Halloween was different now that
she knew that ghosts were not imaginary, witches really did
hide in the shadows, and monsters were real.

She shook her head, jealous of the other children pretending
to be creatures they never suspected walked among them,
scarier than they could imagine, but still—maybe it was best
they didn't know.

She had decided to take Stephen trick-or-treating in the
afternoon so that they could finish up and get to the jamboree
while there was still plenty of light. Coop had hardly smiled
the entire time, often stealing glances over his shoulders. Were
disguised trolls roaming the crowd? Was a witch hiding in the
nearby trees? Only Stephen seemed unaffected by yesterday's
events.

"Total score. I must have a dozen Snickers in here."
Stephen held his candy bag open for Elise and Coop to see.

His makeup had been redone, the filth washed from his
clown costume, and rips in the fabric repaired late into the
night by his sighing but patient mother. She had admonished
Elise to keep a better watch over him tonight while trick-or-
treating. Elise hoped she hadn't noticed how dirty and damp
her own costume had become. Coop had to get a new sheet

altogether.

"Not a bad haul," Coop responded.

"I think we have enough. I say we head for the jamboree," Elise said, pulling a peanut butter cup from Stephen's bag.

"Hey!" Stephen protested.

"Yeah, I'm getting tired of thinking I see Dr. Grout or one of his trolls behind every corner," Coop said.

"Same here." Elise popped the candy into her mouth. "Let's hope they've captured him by now. They said he and his troll were spotted staking out Ms. Hopper's bakery. They're probably hoping to get the cookbook back."

⁂

In the middle of the Eastern Woods, just as Ms. Hopper had described, they came upon a large clearing where the jamboree was already in full swing. A fire burned under a large oak tree. Over the fire hung a black pot encircled by Ms. Hopper, Ms. Thorstad, Bill Black, and several kobolds and elven fairies.

From the oak tree branches hung lit jack-o-lanterns, each with a uniquely carved face. A dozen scarecrows with pumpkin heads hung on spikes near lit torches surrounding the open space.

Above the tree, clouds moved with a life of their own, swirling about in black, grey, and white streaks. Howls and shrieks emanated from them as the sky itself seemed to be bulging to the point of giving way.

"Oh, happity nappity, happy Halloween!" Ms. Hopper exclaimed, tucking the Cookbook under her arm when she spotted Elise and the others.

"There are our little heroes!" Ms. Thorstad added from

the other side of the pot. She winked and then went back to chanting and throwing small metallic looking items into the boiling liquid.

Were those . . . rusty old nails? Elise stared as Ms. Hopper joined in and dropped into the boiling liquid what appeared to be a small knotted rope and some herbs.

"Hi, Ms. Hopper, Ms. Thorstad," Elise said, shifting her gaze from the cauldron to a group of nearby kobolds. Clearly visible, they were adding wood to the fire. The two kobolds they had trapped in the bakery were among them. Elise was relieved that they didn't seem to pay any special attention to her and Coop.

Above them, several elves were crawling along the tree's branches. They were busy relighting jack-o-lanterns blown out by winds from the raucous sky.

"Hello, children," Nigrim squeaked from a high branch.

"Nigrim! Happy Halloween!" Stephen shouted.

"And to you." Nigrim waved and went back to carving a nose into one of the hanging jack-o-lanterns.

"Bill, glad to see you safe," Coop said, smiling at Bill Black, who tipped his wizard's hat in recognition.

"Glad to see you as well. I didn't think you guys could get that book back on your own. Count me as impressed," he said with a grin.

"Did you have trouble with the trolls and Ichabod Crane after we left?" Stephen asked.

"Some. Barely got out of there with my hide intact," Bill said. "Once Ichabod started up another pumpkin bomb, I had to lead him out of there. He and the trolls chased me all the way to the mall doors, but these trolls weren't protected from the light, so they couldn't go outside. Ichabod was too slow to keep up with me, so away I scooted." He smiled at the memory.

"I headed to Hell's Gate to see if I could get to the underground and help, but it was guarded pretty closely. I assume you guys noticed the same on your way out." He nodded toward the pumpkin-headed scarecrows. "Anyway, tonight I'm in charge of the defensive perimeter. Got to stay focused."

"Got it." Stephen peered at the motionless scarecrows, eventually shrugging his shoulders and turning back to the cauldron.

"What are you making?" Elise asked Ms. Hopper, sniffing the rising steam. She hoped she wouldn't have to try it.

"Motion and commotion, it's a potion for our witches' jar to deal with Dr. Grout. Once we have him, we'll give him a dose and shatter the jar. Should break any spells he cast while using the Cookbook and hopefully straighten out his mind." She gave the pot a stir before continuing. "Break his power, won't even take an hour, might taste a little sour." Ms. Hopper smiled and then sprinkled seeds of some sort into the pot, then tossed in a small stone.

"Witches' brew, enchanted stew, Dr. Grout, we're after you!" Ms. Thorstad chanted, waving her arms in the air. She held a long stick that had strands of hay tied to one end.

"A broom!" Coop whispered to Elise.

The kobolds continued tending to the fire while elves and fairies danced in the tree above. Some with wings flew above the chanting witches. It was a marvelous scene, but Elise would feel better if those howling creatures weren't trying to break through the night sky.

"Here they come!" Bill shouted, pointing to the edge of

the surrounding woods.

George First rumbled out of the trees in an old pickup truck with the Plumber riding beside him. The truck bounced over ruts and bumps on an old dirt road before coming to a stop next to the jamboree. As they climbed out, George First put a mask over his face. This time it was a smiling visage with red and yellow streaks.

"Do you have him?" Ms. Thorstad hopped on her stick and floated over to the truck.

"Whoa! They can fly!" Stephen breathed.

"Well, how about that?" Coop said.

"Ms. Hopper, can you do that?" Elise asked. What next?

"I can. Have to be a little careful wareful at my age, but yes."

Ms. Hopper walked over to the pickup, and Elise, Coop, and Stephen followed. Dr. Grout lay on his back in the truck bed with his feet tied together, apparently asleep. James sat next to him. The troll was tied with ropes held by a dozen little men about half the size of the kobolds. They wore scraps of clothes resembling early Native Americans from a past era. Some even wore masks like George First.

Each glanced briefly at the children but then paid them no further mind—until Stephen reached out and patted one of the small men on the head. He jerked his hand back after it hissed and raised a small fist containing a menacing rock.

James let out guttural sounds and strained again against the ropes but could not shake himself free.

"Jogah," Coop whispered. "They're real!"

Some of the small creatures looked at Coop when he spoke the word.

"They are here to take the poisonous creatures back

beneath the earth where they belong," George First said from behind his mask.

"Is Dr. Grout dead?" Stephen asked.

"Passed out from fright. It was quite a task dragging him to the truck and loading him up," the Plumber said, shaking his head.

"I'm not dead and I'm not asleep," Dr. Grout said, struggling to a sitting position. Once upright, he sat with his arms crossed defiantly.

"How did you capture him?" Elise asked.

"We knew he would try and get the Cookbook back from the bakery, so we set a simple trap. Hid a fake book in the walk-in oven and shut him in after he waddled in after the book."

"You should have heard him whimper. I think he thought we were going to cook him like a bad witch." The Plumber laughed, elbowing Dr. Grout in his plump side.

"Savage," Dr. Grout said, shutting his eyes while continuing to sit there with his arms crossed.

"The blubbering coming from the other side of that oven door sure was something," George First added. "And the troll was even easier. We just left out some troll treats, scraps and whatnot, and he followed the trail right to where the jogah were waiting with a large sack to drop on him."

"Sorry about the mess we made over at the shop." The Plumber looked over in Ms. Hopper's direction.

"No problem," she said. "I would expect some mess involved in capturing those two, but we'll get it fixed up in a jiffy wiffy."

"Let's get him up and get on with breaking his spells," Bill said. "We haven't much time." He nodded toward the forest where several sets of glowing eyes peered out from behind trees.

Elise shivered.

It took the might of the group, but they managed to lift Dr. Grout from the truck and deposit him near the cauldron. He did not resist or help; he just accepted the ride, looking around at the burning jack-o-lanterns hanging from the trees and the many elves and kobolds.

"Nice touch with the carved pumpkins." He uncrossed his arms. "What's next?"

"Well, Dr. Grout, I'll tell you what's next." Ms. Hopper dipped a metal ladle into the bubbling pot and poured the liquid into a small glass jar she had produced from within her robes. Elise saw various herbs floating in the jar. She was relieved none of the stones or nails had made it in, even if Dr. Grout deserved them. Still wouldn't taste great, though even without the chunks and debris.

"This is a potion we have been working on all day to keep the spirits at bay," Ms. Hopper said, pointing to the sky. "Also—and this is where you come in, my plump friend—this potion will break any spells, hexes, or bewitchments that had been cast by the one who drinks it. Hopefully, your mind will be restored as well, but no biggie if it isn't." She winked at Elise.

"That's cute but I'm certainly not drinking that." Dr. Grout crossed his arms tighter and clenched his jaw shut.

Ms. Hopper walked over to Dr. Grout, plucked a hair from his head, and dropped it into her jar before twisting the lid shut.

"Ouch!" he yelled.

"Spiddity, biddity, boop." Ms. Hopper began chanting

and waving a hand above her head. "Spiddity, biddity, boop. Spiddity, biddity, boop."

Small sparks began floating up from her fingers. The sparks reached two of the jack-o-lanterns, whose eyes began to blink, their mouths opened wide. They both looked at Dr. Grout and let out a shriek that made Elise shrink backward in terror.

Dr. Grout stared at them, his mouth falling open. Ms. Hopper took the opportunity to pour some of the potion from the jar into his mouth. The kobolds sprang forward and clapped his mouth shut before he could react. He reflexively swallowed the concoction, grabbing at his throat. He then fell flat on his back once more, his eyes closed.

Ms. Hopper replaced the lid on the jar, held it aloft, and chanted, "I send back evil your way three times three. Your bad intentions won't stay, and I return them to you three times three. Your bad intentions won't stay, and I return them to you three times three."

She threw the jar into the fire. It shattered, sending a ball of flame into the air above the cauldron. Stunned, Elise saw the night sky grow noticeably calmer, and some of the spirits flying above quieted or even disappeared.

"When he comes to, his control over the dark folk and the protections from the light he cast upon them will be broken," the Plumber said.

A roar burst from the back of the truck. James the troll began thrashing about. He was able to free a large hand from the jogah. With it, he yanked at the other ropes until he was able to spring free from the truck bed.

"On your guard!" Bill shouted.

Several of the scarecrow heads turned atop the bodies hanging from stakes and the carved eyes blinked to life.

Before they could move further James galloped toward the woods, crashing through the foliage and leaving a ragged tunnel of broken limbs in his wake. The glowing eyes in the forest disappeared as well.

"It seems to be working," The Plumber said, clapping his hands.

"Perhaps it is." Ms. Thorstad landed on the ground and stepped lightly from her broom. "It will take a little while, but it appears that the dark folk have scattered back to the darkness."

Elise and the other children stared off into the woods for awhile absorbing all they had seen before Stephen spoke.

"Is it safe for us to take Mr. Gerald back to the cemetery and release him?" He fished the book on the War of 1812 from his candy bag and held it aloft.

"I think so," Ms. Hopper responded. She looked over her shoulder toward the kobolds. "Jens and Freizen, do you think you can go with them and keep an eye out for any baddies and that troll? I'm sure he's going to keep running until the sun sets, but you never know."

"Yes," the kobolds answered in unison.

"Are they still mad at us?" Elise whispered to Ms. Hopper.

"Hmm, maybe waybe." Ms. Hopper shrugged and went back to stirring the large pot.

Awesome. "Alright, the sun will be setting soon, so let's get on our way," she said to Coop, Stephen, and the two kobolds. She then took flashlights out of her back and handed two to Coop and Stephen who dropped them in their bags.

"Come straight back once Mr. Gerald has been returned to the grave," Ms. Hopper said to the departing group. "Dr.

Grout should be coming around within the next half hour or so, and I don't want you out there in the dark for long tonight."

❧

The Polstein Cemetery wasn't abandoned, but it had had no new burials for years. Although the grounds had been recently cleared of weeds and branches, the surrounding forest was steadily encroaching. It looked to Elise that it would reclaim the carved-out space sooner rather than later.

"Let's spread out and look for Mr. Gerald's grave," Coop said as he turned on his flashlight and started reading the tombstone engravings nearest him. "Yell out when you find something."

The others, including the kobolds, followed his lead, but soon Elise realized that there was a problem.

"Most of these stones are so old that the writing is worn away. There's no way Mr. Gerald's marker will still be legible. Stephen, bring me the War of 1812 book."

As if sensing what Elise was going to do, Stephen opened the book himself and tried to summon Mr. Gerald. It didn't work.

"Give me that," Elise demanded. She uttered the spell, waving her hands as before, and soon enough Mr. Gerald stood at attention before them. The kobolds chattered softly among themselves, the female pointing at Elise, before going back to scouring the woods for any danger.

"Miss Elise. Hello again," Mr. Gerald said with a crisp salute. "I believe my uniform is still damp from our little adventure." He patted at his jacket with his hands and looked down at the dried blood. "Hmm, all that water and it still couldn't get the stain out. Anyway, I see we are back in the old cemetery, we are."

"We figured it was time for you to go home. But we can't find your tombstone," Stephen said.

"Yes, yes. I will admit I am quite tired. Lying down for a rest would be nice." He attempted to stifle a yawn unsuccessfully. He looked about the seemingly random rows of stones and said, "It's back in the far corner, up that way. They buried several of us Brits up there. Bet the gang has been missing me, they have."

"Well, lead the way," Coop said with a smile and salute.

"Don't mind if I do," Mr. Gerald responded.

He led them on a winding path, checking several stones before announcing, "Ah, here it is. Can't miss it."

The marker was no more than a weather-worn square rock with no visible writing remaining. Several other crude markers near Mr. Gerald's made a jagged row.

"There's Mr. Franklin and Mr. Smith and the other boys," Mr. Gerald said, sweeping his arm over several nearby stones.

As he did so, two crows flew above, their sharp caws splitting the sky until they landed on nearby tombstones. Elise could almost swear that the birds were listening to them.

"Well, Mr. Gerald, we will miss you, and we can't thank you enough for all that you did for us," Stephen said. He looked like he was not sure if he should hug the old soldier, salute, or just shake his hand.

"Oh, it was nothing, lad. A lot of fun getting out of the grave once in a while, but I'm getting a little tired, I will admit. How do I get back under anyway? Do we dig up the earth, make another chant?"

"No, simpler than that," Coop said. "Ms. Hopper said all

you have to do is walk across your grave, and that'll do it."

"Hmm, seems simple enough." Mr. Gerald shrugged his shoulders. "Now you children be careful. I don't want you joining me before your time." He looked over at the kobolds. "And you two get them back safely to the others. I sense these woods still hold danger for the living."

The kobolds, now standing hand in hand, nodded their acknowledgment.

"Well now, let's give it a go," Mr. Gerald said, turning toward his grave.

He launched into a smart military march. As he crossed in front of his marker, he started melting into the ground, a little bit of him disappearing with each step until the old ghost vanished completely.

The following moment of silence was broken by the nearby crows. They suddenly took flight, flapping back in the direction from which they had come. The air grew colder as Elise looked up and saw a shadow passing overhead. It was larger than a bird but smaller than a plane. It was the witch— the one with long grey hair from the Goblin Market flying on a broom!

"I don't think she saw us. That was the super creepy one," Stephen whispered as the witch shot across the sky with her robes streaming behind her. "Those birds must have been her spies."

"Figures the kobolds have disappeared," Coop whispered. "Let's get out of here."

Another witch dressed in tattered robes swooped into the sky, her black hair flowing in seeming slow motion behind her. She was scanning the cemetery from right to left. Just before she turned her head in the group's direction, something pulled them down by their ankles behind a cracked crypt. Jens and Freizen, the kobolds, signaled for them to stay quiet.

Please don't see us! Please don't see us! Please don't— But before Elise could finish the thought, goblins, trolls, and other creatures began pouring from the far edge of the wood. It was an army!

Jens pointed in the direction of the jamboree. "Run!" he whispered.

Freizen crawled across the ground in the opposite direction, weaving in and out through the markers until she reached the edge of the wood. 'Hootie hoo!" she yelled at the top of her lungs.

Trolls and goblins stopped where they were, and the witches turned on their brooms.

"There!" the gray-haired witch screamed in a voice that grated like rocks scraping together.

The black-haired witch swooped down toward the little kobold, and Elise stood frozen as Freizen ran off into the woods with several goblins in pursuit.

"Go!" Jens urged again, pointing in the direction of the jamboree. He then dashed in the direction of the monsters instead of away as he had directed the others.

"Come on, we have to go!" Coop grabbed both Elise and Stephen by the arms, and once again, before Elise could barely comprehend what was happening, she was running without daring to look back.

CHAPTER SIXTEEN

The Battle of Legend Hollow

Elise sprinted after the others down a faint animal track that looked like it had not been used in ages. Behind her, something was crashing through the underbrush, branches snapping, while the cackles of the witches made the hair on the back of her neck stand up.

Where were they? Elise looked up and saw the witches splitting the night sky just above the trees. Their capes and ragged robes rustled fiercely in the wind. The grey witch flew ahead before turning her broom handle downward and diving at Coop.

"Coop!" Her mouth was so dry, Elise could barely scream his name. It was enough for Coop to duck, and Stephen did the same.

The grey witch missed them both, nearly smashing into a

low-hanging branch. She shrieked with anger and turned her broom once more. Elise's heart jumped to her throat. The witch was now aiming for her!

She swung behind a nearby tree, closing her eyes. All sound seemed to stop, and Elise squeezed her eyes tighter shut until a foul odor hit her nostrils, shocking her eyes open. Her blood went cold as she stared directly into the red eyes of the grey witch hovering mere feet away, smiling a horrible cracked-tooth smile.

Elise screamed as the grey witch cackled and lunged at her. Wrapping her arms over her head, Elise dove to the ground. She felt a single nail from the witch's hand scratch her arm, leaving a burning mark as the creature flew back over the trees.

No sooner had the witch flown away than more terrible sounds came to Elise's ears. The trolls came stomping through the brush, growling with rage. Elise peered out through her fingers and saw what she thought were flying monkeys passing through the treetops.

No—they were goblins jumping from limb to limb, but some actually did have wings. Another witch led them, this one dressed in black rags and wearing a crooked black hat. A real Halloween witch, Elise thought numbly. The black witch raised her hand and began chanting. She hovered above Elise and the others until her hand glowed red, her eyes just slits and a cruel smile splitting her wicked face.

"Keep running!" Coop yelled.

He grabbed Elise by the hand but then yanked his own back just as quickly. "Ow! Your hand feels like it's on fire!"

Elise looked down in horror. The witch's mark was now oozing puss. A wave of pain coursed through her arm and hand. Did the witch poison her? She scrambled to her feet, trying to ignore the burning ache.

"No time to deal with this. We need to get to Ms. Hopper and the rest of the Society. Go!"

Coop's brow furrowed, but Elise shoved at him. No time, she thought again as the dark mob closed in. The three ran down the trail.

The black witch swooshed above them. Elise flung a glance up at her just as she stopped chanting. She pointed in their direction, and as they ran, tree limbs began to slap at them, bushes leaned in to scratch at their legs, and vines grabbed and tore at their clothing.

Elise struggled against the unnatural forces. She felt like she was running through quicksand as the forest tried to stop their progress and hold them fast. The path was endless and they ran forever as the monsters drew closer no matter how much they tried to get away.

Elise's lungs were on the verge of bursting when they finally reached the clearing with the jamboree still going full tilt. Ahead, the Plumber and Ms. Hopper had Dr. Grout up and standing between them though he still seemed to be asleep.

Elise and the others dashed forward, waving their arms in the air and yelling.

"Oh, baddity raddity," Ms. Hopper cried. "What is it, children?"

"It didn't work!" Stephen shouted.

"What didn't work?" The Plumber asked, still holding the plump arm of Dr. Grout.

"The potion!" Elise yelled, trying to catch her breath. "It didn't work. They're all still under his control! They're coming!"

Ms. Hopper and the others looked confused.

"Look," Elise said, rolling up her sleeve. "The grey witch left her mark on me just now."

"Oh, no, no, no, that is no good." Miss Hooper grabbed the Cookbook, flipped to a page somewhere near the middle, and began reading aloud from the page.

"B-but," George First stammered. Before he could continue, the grey and black witches came swooping out of the sky, goblins poured from the trees, and several trolls led by James came crashing through the vegetation.

"Keep them back and away from Dr. Grout!" Ms. Hopper shouted. "Elise, come with me to the tree."

Elise hurried after her. Ms. Hopper began again reading from the page. She then grabbed Elise's arm, knocked on the tree three times, tore off a leaf, clapped it between her hands, and rubbed it on Elise's wound while shouting out, "Hither come, hither go, you are not welcome, so grey witch and all your bewitchments, go!" She repeated the chant three times before releasing Elise's arm.

Elise cried out in pain as Ms. Hopper's hand pulled away but then gawked as the mark faded and disappear. She opened her mouth to thank Ms. Hopper, but there was no time— everyone around her seemed to be moving at once as the dark creatures surged toward them.

The pumpkin-headed scarecrows gangly arms sprang to life, unhooking themselves from the wood crosses from which they hung. Once their feet found the ground, they formed a circle around the October Society and the jack-o-lantern– covered tree.

Elise's head whirled as Ms. Hopper and Ms. Thorstad began chanting more incantations while the kobolds grabbed small knives, hammers and even shovels from their belts. The jogah scrambled to places of ambush under piles of leaves while the fairies who perched in the tree held tiny bows at the ready.

As the dark army approached, the scarecrows engaged. Their arms and legs jerked stiffly as they grabbed squealing goblins by the handful. They threw them back toward the trees where the creatures tumbled shrieking to the ground.

They had less lucky with the trolls. The powerful monsters shook loose of the scarecrows' grasp and tore them limb from limb. Straw flew through the air, and several pumpkin heads rolled upon the ground in front of their damaged bodies.

Elise felt sick watching the scarecrows fall one after another, but then a strange thing happened. The scattered limbs and torsos of the scarecrows began coming back together. Their ragged bodies staggered about, replacing limbs and gathering pumpkin heads from the ground to plunk them back in place as good as new.

"Wow!" Stephen exclaimed.

As many times as the trolls would rip the scarecrows apart, they would reform and join the fight once again. The trolls began to grow exhausted, and Ms. Hopper took advantage of the precious time they bought by opening the Cookbook and preparing another spell. She picked up a stone from the ground, held it aloft, and chanted, "Hobbly knobbly and stitches and moans. Take a troll's bones and turn them to stone!"

She then pointed the hand holding the stone at the nearest troll, one Elise recognized from the arcade. Bolts of orange rays shot from her fingers. They exploded in a blast so bright that it lit up the sky above the troll as if it was day.

The troll screamed and froze where it stood. Its skin turned grey, then white and craggy. He was turning to stone! Elise exhaled in relief, but then the process stopped and the troll turned back to flesh, launching its attacks once more.

"Oh me, oh my! They're still under protection," Ms. Hopper exclaimed while flipping quickly through the pages of the Cookbook. "I must find the right spell to break it." Her page-flipping became more urgent as she continued to mumble to herself.

"I don't understand why I can't find it. Oh, hobbly nobbly, my age is catching up to me. My memory is going. I know that spell was here." Ms. Hopper's hair tower bobbed about as her search continued.

The grey witch flew above, carrying a torch. She threw it toward a scarecrow and hissed through her crooked teeth as it missed bouncing away harmlessly.

The black witch threw a second torch, and her aim was true. A spark near the scarecrow's shoulder began to smolder until finally, a small flame erupted. The scarecrow patted at the flame, but it was too late. The fire spread quickly, and soon the straw-stuffed figure was reduced to just a pile of ash on the ground topped by a burnt pumpkin.

The witches swooped low to gather more sticks from the trees for torches, but the sky around them swarmed with dozens of tiny arrows let loose by the fairies and elves. The witches screamed out in pain as their skin began to bristle with the tiny missiles. They retreated to the safety of the skies high above the forest.

Through all of the chaos, Ms. Hopper continued her frantic search through the Cookbook. Stephen and Coop huddled with Elise as the battle raged around them. A group of jogah sprang from a hole in the ground, dragging a net they used to capture an unsuspecting goblin. The green-skinned creature thrashed about, its sharp teeth tearing at the netting. The goblin and the jogah group tumbled and rolled about until they bounced right into the Plumber and the still sleeping Dr. Grout.

"What? Where am I? What is happening?" Dr. Grout exclaimed, suddenly awake. The look of confusion on his face gave way to understanding. He struggled with the Plumber, who held on tightly. "James, to me!" he shouted at the large troll leading the other dark creatures in the nearby tumult.

James ignored his command, and Dr. Grout shouted again, but the results were the same. Dr. Grout next tried commanding some nearby goblins, but they also paid no attention to him.

"Why do they ignore me?" Dr. Grout asked, turning to Ms. Thorstad. She was dipping a jar into the cauldron, filling it with small twigs and rocks along with the potion. She took the jar and quickly buried it nearby in the soft soil before mounting her broom.

Dr. Grout looked about, clearly exasperated. His eyes widened when he saw Ms. Hopper holding the Cookbook. Elise shrank back, pulling Coop and Stephen with her.

"Why does she have the book and not you?" he shouted to Ms. Thorstad, who swung around to turn her gaze on the now panicking man.

"Shut up, you fool!" she hissed.

"Me shut up!" Dr. Grout tried to pull free again from the Plumber. "You said that if I secured that book, you would get Ms. Hopper out of the bakery. Well, it appears she is not only still around but she once again has the Cookbook in her possession. I did my part, yet here I am!" Dr. Grout stomped his foot on the ground.

What? Elise looked back and forth between Dr. Grout and Ms. Thorstad. Ms. Hopper's friend was . . . a traitor?

Ms. Thorstad appeared to be struggling with a response. She gazed back for a moment, then simply shrugged her shoulders.

"Enough of this charade." She pointed her broom toward Ms. Hopper, swooping down and reaching for the Cookbook.

"No!" Elise jumped to Ms. Hopper's side, knocking Ms. Thorstad off course. She retreated to the skies as the grey witch flew over, looking down upon Elise. Before Elise could look away, the grey witch narrowed her eyes and squeezed her fist. Elise's arm began to burn again where the mark had been.

"Argh!" She fell to the ground, squirming until the grey witch flew away and the pain subsided.

"There are still traces of the poison, but it will pass soon, sweetie," Ms. Hopper assured Elise, helping her up.

"The book should have been mine," Ms. Thorstad shouted, slowly circling above. "I mean, using it to make pastries, really! We have witches to avenge, power to secure, and the natural world at our fingertips. Dumplings and cupcakes?" She swooped off toward James and the other trolls who were still battling the indefatigable scarecrows.

"Destroy the heads, James! Destroy the pumpkin heads, and they can't reform." She curved back around, joined by the black and grey witches. "Not that hard to figure out, really."

James stood still for a moment, appearing to ponder Ms. Thorstad's words before lashing out and grabbing the arm of a scarecrow. He ripped it from its socket and tossed it behind him. He then grabbed the pumpkin from atop the stuffed body, smashed it to the ground, and brutally stomped it into small pieces.

Several elves squealed at the sight, and nearby kobolds chittered and shook their heads. The trolls roared with approval and began smashing nearby pumpkin heads. Headless scarecrow bodies dropped senseless to the ground. Elise could barely watch, and Coop groaned beside her. The tide of the battle had turned.

"We must stop them!" Bill shouted. "We can handle the goblins and keep the witches at bay, but without the scarecrows, I don't know if we can hold out much longer against the trolls!"

"Shoot, newt, doot." Ms. Hopper continued to page through the Cookbook. "I can't find the protection spell for the trolls so I can reverse it. I know it's in here—I've used it in the past myself."

"Oh, do you mean this page?" Ms. Thorstad shouted from above, waving a scrap of paper. "I took the liberty of tearing it from the book after it was recovered from the Goblin Market. I figured a little insurance with the trolls would come in handy."

The grey and black witches hovered and cackled at her side as the trolls redoubled their efforts on the ground. The entire October Society were squeezed into a small circle with their backs nearly pressed against the black cauldron and the giant tree. Elise grabbed Coop's and Stephen's hands. If they were going to go down, they'd go down together.

The sky above the tree swirled and raged. Several more spirits slipped through from the beyond. They screamed and wailed with both delight and fury, filling Elise with cold horror. Many of the elves and fairies stopped firing their tiny arrows and instead sought shelter within the hollow spaces of the giant tree.

"Don't worry, it's going to be fine," Stephen announced in a calm, unwavering voice.

"How can you say that? Look around you!" Elise shouted back.

"I am looking." Stephen pointed to a far branch of the giant tree.

Elise followed his finger. A kobold was crawling on a limb extending from the tree. The limb nearly reached where Ms. Thorstad and the witches hovered. Tiny Nigrim crouched on the kobold's back, holding his firework lantern.

The witches, distracted by the destruction of the scarecrows and the spirits pouring forth from the sky, failed to notice the kobold or Nigrim. The elf handed his lantern to the kobold who then reared his arm back and threw the lantern at the witches with all of his might.

The sound of shattering glass filled the air as the lantern struck the grey witch. She cried out as the firework spark bounced off her harmlessly but landed in the folds of the nearby black witch's robe. Almost immediately, the tattered garment burst into flame, igniting the straw of her broom as well.

The black witch screamed and shrank from the fire. She flew upward and downward and in circles but could not escape her burning robes and broom.

The other witches watched with mouths agape and did not think to flee until their panicked coven mate flew into them blindly, spreading the flames. They shrieked as the black witch skittered away above the treetops. Teetering on her broom,

Ms. Thorstad dropped the Cookbook page, which fluttered toward the ground.

She gathered herself and pointed her broom downward toward the page in its butterfly flight. It landed on the ground before she could reach it. She leaped from her broom, but just as she reached for the page, dozens of jogah burst from their hiding holes and held her fast, leaving her screeching with rage.

George First let out a victory whoop. He grabbed the page and handed it to Ms. Hopper.

"Come read with me, child," Ms. Hopper said to Elise. "I need all of the strength I can muster."

"I-I—" Elise stammered.

"Now!" Ms. Hopper said.

"OK!" Elise ran to her side.

"Good. Now, the spell on this page protects the trolls from their weakness, which is the light of the day. I am going to cast a reversal using the original spell itself. Follow along with me."

All around them goblins and kobolds battled and squealed, trolls tore scarecrows asunder, and the October Society fought on. Ms. Hopper did her best to ignore the chaos as she read from the page until suddenly, she extended her left hand upwards.

"A cup of the potion, please, and into it put a sun-fed leaf from a tree, a flower kissed by a bee, and the breath of a child, perhaps one sometimes called Steve." Ms. Hopper winked at Stephen.

Coop grabbed a metal cup lying near the cauldron and filled it from the steaming pot. Nigrim pulled a leaf from the tree and dropped it in while a kobold picked a nearby black-eyed Susan flower and floated it atop the concoction. Then all eyes turned to Stephen.

"Well, nobody calls me Steve, but here we go." Stephen took the cup from Coop, drew in a large breath, and exhaled into the cup before handing it to Ms. Hopper.

"That should do, that should do." She placed the cup on the ground and kneeled next to it. She breathed deeply twice before closing her eyes and beginning to chant.

"Creatures of the night with all your might, you shall fall victim once more to the bright. Nightily, brightily, light!"

She looked over at Elise. "Now join me!"

Elise trembled, watching another scarecrow fall, but she sat down next to Ms. Hopper. She could do this. She could do this!

"Creatures of the night with all your might, you shall fall victim once more to the bright. Nightily, brightily, light!" Ms. Hopper chanted once more. Elise only got about half of the words right and shook her head. Come on, Elise!

"Creatures of the night with all your might, you shall fall victim once more to the bright. Nightily, brightily, light!" This time Elise got it right and felt herself falling into the rhythm of the chant.

On the fourth time through, a strange sensation swelled within Elise. It was like an energy swirling through her limbs and coming together as a ball in her chest. The feeling moved to her fingertips and came out as streaks of light. What was happening?

"Easy, sweetie, you're doing great," Ms. Hopper said..

The same streaks of light were exploding from Ms. Hopper's fingers. The streaks floated above them and joined together into a huge globe of light illuminating the sky near them.

The trolls stopped attacking the few remaining scarecrows. Some stared above at the nearly blinding light while others turned and ran for the forest, but none made it far. Their skin turned grey with jagged lines, and moments later they had transformed into large boulders, mounds of dirt, and even small hills.

"Gone, gone, you are no more strong!" Ms. Hopper shouted. "Great job, Elise. You may make a proper witch one day." She said with a wink.

The goblins screamed in terror even as the light began to fade. They fell into full retreat, sprinting from the clearing back into the woods while the grey and black witches let loose angry shrieks, flying off into the sky.

The swirling clouds above the pumpkin-covered tree slowed their chaotic motions, and the opening in the night sky began to close. As it shrank, it sucked in the banshees and spirits that had broken through during the night, spitting them back to the other side. With a quiet whoosh, the hole closed and vanished.

The exhausted fairy folk cheered, and the October Society breathed a collective sigh of relief.

"I mean, what a second date. I didn't think we could top the first." Coop said taking Elise's hand while still panting from the exertion. Elise laughed and squeezed his hand back.

"Hey, over there!" Stephen shouted. He pointed toward the edge of the wood where Dr. Grout had managed to trundle off during the final throes of the battle.

"He's getting away!" Coop said, dropping Elise's hand.

"He won't get far." Bill had fallen to his knees with exhaustion, but he smiled. "We'll gather him up tomorrow.

Either way, any power he gained from the Cookbook and Ms. Thorstad is now broken. He can't do much harm at this point." He took his wizard hat from his head and wiped the sweat from his face.

"What's more, earlier I cast a hex upon him for good measure," Ms. Hopper added with a hint of a smile. "His luck is about to change."

"And what about me?" Ms. Thorstad asked, still immobilized by the jogah.

"Welly nelly, you will be taken before the High Council in New York City." Ms. Hopper let out a deep breath. "I will say that I am disappointed, Ellen. You being my fellow coven member and all, and I thought we were friends. I expected more from you."

"Oh, whatever," Ms. Thorstad responded, rolling her eyes. "I just wanted the book. I knew you wouldn't give it up willingly. I'm getting older, and I deserve a turn. As I said, you weren't doing anything important with it."

"I was making people happy, and I think that is very important," Ms. Hopper said, folding her arms. "And I plan to put it back to good use as early as tomorrow morning." She smiled at Elise. "We've got some serious baking to do and a critic to please, after all."

EPILOGUE

From the journal of Niles Folsom, High Doctor, October Society of
New York City
Commentary Regarding the Happenings in Legend Hollow, New
York

Monday, November 24, 1986, Legend Hollow, New York

*I*n the days since the battle of Legend Hollow on All Hallows
Eve, the townspeople have no longer been subjected to screams
in the night, dark witches in flight, or trolls roaming in the light.
What remains of the November Men have gone to ground to lick
their wounds, and Ms. Thorstad will soon stand trial before the
High Council in New York City.

The Cookbook is secure once more in Ms. Hopper's possession,
but at some point, protection of the powerful tome will have to
pass to another. That, thankfully, is a decision for another day,
and for now we will concentrate on the fact that the barrier

between the two worlds has been preserved and order brought once again to Legend Hollow.

It was one day until Thanksgiving, and the line of customers snaked out the bakery door and halfway down the block. People were desperate to obtain some of the magical desserts they had heard everyone rave about, maybe take a box home for their special holiday dinners. Elise tried to keep the customers in order while Lilah herded the crowd, barking orders.

It had been three weeks since the newspaper critic's glowing review, but people had started showing up right away. They came gradually at first but built each day and were now a happy mob stomping their feet to keep warm, waiting patiently out in the cold.

Elise's mother and Stephen sat in a nearby booth, enjoying a pile of Pumpkin Spice Pilgrim's Hat cookies and Kobold's Delight donuts. The redeemed Mr. Hernandez appeared from the back room, carrying trays under his good arm, and Ms. Hopper danced behind the main counter, filling orders with a flourish.

How much her father would have loved seeing the bakery returned to its glory! Elise took comfort in the thought that he had been right about Washington Irving visiting the town. He had been right about a lot of things, and she'd never be able to tell him.

She pushed the thought away. This day was meant for happy thoughts. She smiled as she handed her customer his box of treats, then took a break to sit down at the table with her family and a donut.

Bill Black entered the shop, pushing through the crowds

until he was behind the display counter next to Ms. Hopper. He took off his wizard hat, took a folded piece of paper from it, and handed it to her.

Ms. Hopper finished packing up a box before sliding on her glasses and reading the letter. Elise munched her crumbly donut and watched Bill. Even for him, this behavior seemed odd. What was up? Between bites of her dessert, she kept an eye on Ms. Hopper while Bill fidgeted nervously.

Elise put down her unfinished donut when she saw a concerned expression spread across Ms. Hopper's face. When she finished the letter, she placed it on the counter and turned her gaze right back on Elise.

The donut rumbled uncomfortably in her stomach. Ms. Hopper motioned her over with her finger.

"I'll be right back," Elise said to her mom and Stephen.

Mr. Hernandez took over with the customers while Ms. Hopper took Elise to the back room. Bill followed, and they sat at the work table.

"Oh, noogedly googedly," Ms. Hopper said. "I have concerning but, I think, ultimately good news. Please read this letter we just received from New York." She slid the letter over to Elise.

Her stomach fluttering, Elise picked it up.

November 23, 1986

Dear Ms. Hopper,

A new disturbance seems to be rising from the depths below New York City. Tunnel-dwelling kobolds have passed along several observations, and one of them I thought would be of particular interest to you.

They have reported seeing a prisoner of some importance in bondage and under strict guard. Follow-up investigations by the October Society have given rise to the suspicion that the prisoner is none other than the lost archivist and historian of the Legend Hollow October Society, one Mr. Terry Wood, the father of Elise and Stephen Wood.

The reports state that although he was alive, he did not appear to be in good health. The dark folk are exposing him to torment to extract Washington Irving's secrets, the location of the Society's tomes of knowledge, and anything else that they can coax from him regarding headless horsemen and subjects of import.

We don't know how he came to be in their possession, but a rescue will be planned immediately. Considering the extraordinary performance of Mr. Wood's children during the Legend Hollow Cookbook incident, I have sent an envoy to gather them and enlist their assistance in this important rescue. I will post again as soon as I have more updates, but until the envoy arrives, please relay this information to those who need to know.

Niles Folsom
High Doctor
October Society, New York City Chapter

Elise read the letter a second time, her heart pounding, before raising her eyes to Ms. Hopper's gaze. Dad was alive! She then turned her gaze to her mom and Stephen in the front room still enjoying their donuts. And me and the October Society are going to bring him home!

TAYLOR PENSONEAU is the author of the Legend Hollow series. He is originally from Illinois, was a longtime resident of Colorado and now resides in Florida with his wonderful wife Pamela and their two daughters Lana and Elise. Taylor is an avid cyclist, snowboarder, IPA enthusiast, fisherman and lover of legend and lore.

If you have enjoyed this book, please share a brief positive review on Amazon and Goodreads so that others may also enjoy it. Just go to **linktr.ee/legendhollowauthor** and follow the review links. Thank you so much in advance!

Made in the USA
Monee, IL
28 November 2023

47507539R00114